THE

NECESSARY

ANGEL

C.K. STEAD

ALLEN&UNWIN

First published in Australia in 2017 by Allen & Unwin
First published in Great Britain in 2018 by Allen & Unwin

This paperback edition published in Great Britain in 2018 by Allen & Unwin

Allen & Unwin
c/o Atlantic Books Ltd
Ormond House
26–27 Boswell Street
London WC1N 3JZ

Telephone: 020 7269 1610
Fax: 020 7430 0916
E-mail: UK@allenandunwin.com
Website: www.allenandunwin.com/uk

A CIP catalogue record for this book is available from the British Library.

Design by Kate Barraclough
Set in 12.5/18 pt Adobe Garamond Pro

Paperback ISBN: 978 1 76063 116 1
E-book ISBN: 978 1 76063 823 8

Printed in Great Britain by
Clays Ltd, Elcograf S.p.A.

10 9 8 7 6 5 4 3 2 1

THE

NECESSARY

ANGEL

To Claire Davison
and to Margaret Stead

Note: It can be assumed that most of the conversations in this novel are in French, except where the text (or common sense) suggests otherwise.

I.

SUMMER

2014

1.

MIDSUMMER

NIGHT

THEY WERE CLOSE TO THE end of their meal and their meeting when Max Jackson commented on the noise coming from the street.

'It's the twenty-first of June,' Sylvie said—and he had to shift his thoughts from the practical matters they'd been talking about to register what this meant: midsummer's night—the streets would soon be full of revellers, musicians, rock groups, *fêtards*.

He smiled and put a hand on her arm. It was a way of saying, 'Of course—I'd forgotten.' He glanced at her face and she smiled.

The others were gathering up their papers, handbags, silk wraps and scarves. He signalled with his credit card. It was at the expense of the Sorbonne Nouvelle—that was understood, and he would deal with it.

There were farewells, thanks, promises of 'further suggestions along the same lines'—the kind of winding down and wrapping up when progress has been made. The next stage, the *doing*, might be more difficult. In the meantime they had a plan. Exactly a year from now, the weekend of 19 to 21 June 2015, there would be a conference, or perhaps something on a slightly smaller scale, what was sometimes called in France a *journée d'études*, which would focus on just eight poets—four English, four French—who had been killed in battle, or died of wounds in the 1914–18 war, the centenary of which was currently being commemorated. It would be a memorialisation of the fallen, but a literary one; and keeping the number of writers down meant there was some chance of keeping the academic standard up. To Max it felt like a small but significant triumph. And somehow it had been achieved despite very good wine, and Le Procope's 'famous *coq au vin traditionnel*' preceded by *barigoule de légumes*, and followed by cheeses and fruit.

Despite—or because of? Either way it had happened, it was done, and he was pleased—with himself and with his colleagues, who had seemed to go out of their way to avoid old arguments. This was Paris, and one of its most venerable cafés, where (as it liked to boast) 'Balzac, Hugo, Verlaine and so many others' had planned their books and argued about them, dazzling their friends and admirers, throwing dust in the eyes of their enemies and detractors. Max, who had lived in Paris long enough to feel at ease if not at home, understood all this, and paid these venerable walls and decorated ceilings at least the lip service they expected, and sometimes the more-than-lip service they probably deserved. Now his mind was elsewhere—or nowhere, except in the satisfaction of something accomplished, and the warm and welcome proximity of Sylvie Renard, a recent addition to his Department of Comparative Literature.

The short, plump, pompous young expert on Apollinaire, whose name Max had not caught or couldn't now remember, was still talking. There was so much yet to be said about Apollinaire, he was insisting, so much only now emerging from the years spent in Nice. It was true he had not died in battle—it was the Spanish flu that had taken him off two days before the Armistice was signed. But he'd been trepanned for shrapnel wounds and that must have weakened his resistance. He could certainly have been honoured as one *mort pour la patrie*—and indeed was, in the street named after him, and by the tombstone in Père Lachaise.

He had said this already, more than once, and no one now was paying attention. He looked to Max (whose knowledge of Apollinaire was limited) for agreement, for confirmation, and Max nodded and tried to look keen. 'Sure. Yes—he's one of our eight. That's almost certain, I think. And, yes, the Nice years especially.'

Sylvie stood beside him at the desk. There was some rechecking of the bill being done, a small correction to be made. There was a spider's web, low down almost out of sight where a cleaner would easily miss it. With the tip of his biro, Max touched it. Instantly the insect began to spin in fast circles, violently shaking its web. He said, 'I always wonder what they're doing when they do that.'

'Panic,' Sylvie said.

'Yes, but what's going on exactly?'

'Hiding the money,' she suggested.

He laughed. 'A raid, d'you think?'

'Monsieur.' The card was returned, with a modest flourish and polite thanks, not excessive, because this was, after all, Le Procope, and who owed most thanks—the famous location or its customer?

They walked down the stairs together, Sylvie and Max. As they pushed out through the doors into that huge, raucous crush of people filling the street like a swollen river from one bank to the other, she grabbed his hand—or had he taken hers?—so they would not be swept away from one another on the current.

They fought their way out of the rue de l'Ancienne Comédie and across the boulevard. She was leading the way now and he followed, veering right, battered by the racket, the kinds of noise changing from moment to moment. He was uncertain now where they were, where they were going, and didn't care so long as his hand was in hers.

When she stopped he thought he recognised they were in the rue de Vaugirard. People still swirled around them and they were buffeted this way and that. 'It's like the end of *Les Enfants du Paradis*,' he said but she didn't hear.

'The movie,' he shouted.

She pointed to her ears and shook her head. 'Come,' she said, pulling him with the left hand that was still holding his wrist, and with the other punching a number code in at the door from the street.

Inside, when the door was shut on the wild out-there world, she said, 'Have you got a moment? Come up—I couldn't hear a word.'

He would not have suggested this himself but was glad of it. It removed a barrier. While they waited for the lift, '*Les Enfants du Paradis*,' he repeated. 'That's what I was shouting at you. Classic French movie. Ends with Jean-Louis Barrault losing the woman he loves in a crowd . . . I'm probably telling you something you know.'

'Garance,' she wailed, imitating Barrault's lament. '*Garance!*'

Oh, so she had been listening—and of course she knew the movie. How could she not?

Sylvie smiled at him as the cage cranked down to them. The doors opened. As they entered the small space, he thought of asking whether there was a man in her life, but it was one of those thoughts rejected before spoken. She would probably answer 'Of course', or 'Always', leaving him no better informed, and mildly punished for being the predictable male in a Paris lift. And she would not need to ask if he had a wife because she would know from talk in the department that there was one, of long standing, French, that they were 'somewhat estranged' (Max's own description of their present arrangement), and that there were two children.

On the other hand, maybe she had heard nothing, had not been interested enough even to enquire. In the past few days the beautiful, clever, intuitive (as she seemed to him) Sylvie Renard had taken hold of his imagination as firmly as she had just taken his hand in the street.

They stepped out at the sixth floor. A light came on. Sylvie approached the apartment door, tucking something under one arm and hunting for keys in her bag. She asked, 'Would you like coffee?'

'That would be nice . . .'

'A small noisette?'

'Thank you.'

He hummed a few bars of a tune he'd heard out there on the street, nervous while she fiddled at the lock. She opened the door. There were lights on in there. 'Darling, it's me,' she called ahead of herself.

And there was a response half heard—a male voice, a deep rumble.

•

AND, AS FOR SYLVIE, HER hand gripping his in that crossing of two major and some minor thoroughfares, through the almost-meltdown of the normal order of things, which was not a real meltdown because the fact of it, and its limits, were what the season and the day of the year dictated: the head-banging racket of it all, the beating her ears were taking—different songs, different voices and languages, klaxons, firecrackers, the seasonal euphoria, the urban cacophony. She was glad to have hold of him, grateful for his physical nearness, yet surprised, and even, dimly, displeased, that he should have signalled interest in her so unambiguously during the whole of their dinner, and now, alone with her, even in this undisciplined moment, seemed unwilling or unable to turn wish into action. Why so passive? Should she reproach herself for the same half-step forward and half-step back? Possibly, probably, yes and no. He was her senior, after all; but it was her impulse now that was pulling him indoors out of the crowd, inviting him to come up to where they could look down on it all, as if on themselves, from above, and where he could learn a little about her in answer to the questions he did not, and probably would not, ask. He had not intended to be heard telling her, as they emerged into the street, that she was beautiful, but chancing it—and of course she had heard, or thought she had. Why even now did he not kiss her in the lift, since it was what he wanted, and what she might welcome—how could they know if he didn't try? So they were going up, rising above the racket, and he was trying to impress her by talking about *Les Enfants du Paradis*, that tired old classic of French cinema. Yes, the wine at Le Procope had been good and she'd had enough of it to say what fierce, unbridled things needed to be said, and to do what wild Midsummer Night things needed to be done, if only she and Max could be alone together . . .

But there were lights on in there.

'Darling, it's me,' she called.

AT THE DOOR MAX WAS making the necessary inner adjustment. His feelings were mixed—disappointment, but also relief. He would not be called upon to be decisive—only sociable. Or did this only add an extra dimension to what might still be an adventure and a challenge? Signals, you could say, had gone back and forth between him and Sylvie—or he thought they had. They might come to mean little or a lot.

'Come in,' she said. 'He'll be pleased to meet you.'

And there he was, scrambling up out of his armchair. He had a lot of frizzy-blond, somewhat grizzled hair standing out from his head as though electrified. Solidly built—a sort of Beethoven figure, robust but not beautiful. Middle-aged—possibly older than Max, but not much. Max smiled, amused as he told himself, 'Someone got here before you.' He felt relaxed, relieved of an anxiety.

'Max, this is Bertholdt Volker. And his English is better than his French, so you can speak to him in English if you prefer.'

But they continued in French. 'Bertholdt's a TV producer,' Sylvie explained. 'France 5. Canal.'

'Max,' Bertholdt said, shaking his hand. 'Professor Jackson. I've heard good things about you.'

'I too—likewise,' Max said, though in fact he'd heard nothing.

She gathered up papers that were scattered about the coffee table and the sofa, tidying them into a single sheaf. 'Will you do coffee for us, Bertholdt? You make it so much better.' And then to Max, 'He doesn't like my coffee. He's very particular. Come and look at the apartment.'

Already Max was taking in the view from the windows—down there the Luxembourg Gardens, in darkness now the gates had closed for the night, but the palace illuminated for Midsummer Night.

'Lovely in the daytime,' she said; and told him about this interior space, under the slope of the mansards, that had been created by converting the servants' quarters—*les chambres de bonnes*—taking out partitions. The floors were polished wood with good-quality woollen rugs. On a low square table were ceramic bowls, a spiky flower arrangement and a piece of carved greenstone. A Matisse lithograph on the wall was of a woman in red wearing a grey-blue hat; another was a poster for a Fernand Léger exhibition, in dark blue. On the bookshelves the books looked very handsome, possibly more looked at than read. The walls were dark grey and pale yellow. The piano at the far end of the room was an ordinary upright, pale grey rather than the usual dark brown. The screen at the far end was a big one. The sofa was Danske Møbler, with no back support: you either perched there, or you lay down. The glossy magazines—arts, architecture, gardens, cooking—were in an angled holder on the floor at the end of the sofa. 'It's Bertholdt's apartment,' Sylvie said, noticing his eye on the magazines.

'It's very nice,' Max said. 'And you're a pianist. I saw it on your CV.'

'I was, yes. Past tense. But it used to be serious, so it goes into the record.'

'Please—play something.'

'Not on this piano,' she said. 'It's here as part of the décor but he doesn't have it tuned.' She struck one note, and then a pair, by way of illustration. It sounded fine to Max.

'Another time,' she said. 'Not here, not now.'

He said, 'I'll hold you to that.'

The small strong coffees were served with a little jug of hot milk on the side. 'Add according to taste,' Bertholdt said.

Sylvie perched beside Max. Bertholdt sprawled in his chair and explained how it was that he was working on a production of *The Ghost Sonata* for Canal. 'There was a famous production of it done not long after Strindberg died—by Max Reinhardt in Berlin. I suspect that's why they asked me to do it. Thought, Germans can make sense of this mad Swede. Let's give it to Bertholdt. He'll make it work.'

'And have you?'

'It's fiendishly difficult—just to make sense of it. It keeps me awake at night.'

'Keeps us both awake,' she said.

Bertholdt asked how the dinner had gone and between them Max and Sylvie explained how far the meeting had taken them. 'It's a start,' Max said.

'A rather expensive one,' Sylvie said.

'Another Great War centennial,' Bertholdt said. 'By the time we get to November 2018 we're going to be tired of them.'

'Today, however,' Sylvie said, 'is June 2014. Let's not be tired in advance.'

Bertholdt asked about Max's career, how it had brought him to France.

'My wife, Louise, is French. I came here to do postgraduate work—we were students together, and we . . .'

'Married,' Sylvie said, exploiting his hesitation.

Max said, 'That's the shortened version, yes.'

'And children?'

'Girl and boy, eight and twelve. Two small Frogs.'

'Bilingual?' Bertholdt asked.

'Of course. No detectable accent, but French is definitely the mother tongue.'

Feeling the old, familiar need to explain further he said, 'I'm not English. I came here from London, but I was born in New Zealand. Grew up there.'

'Unimaginable,' Bertholdt said; and when Max looked as if he did not understand, Bertholdt said, 'Such a long way.'

'You have to start somewhere,' Max said; and then, 'You have a piece of pounamu.'

Bertholdt looked where he was pointing. 'It's jade, isn't it?'

'Jade, greenstone—the Māori word is pounamu.'

Bertholdt's sideways nod of the head was an unspoken 'Whatever'.

'So, in the family,' Sylvie said, 'you're the outsider.'

'I'm the foreigner—downstairs with the dog.'

'Downstairs—really?'

'We have two apartments. They both belong to Louise—to her family. Her father was a distinguished civil servant—*Légion d'Honneur* and so on. An earlier forebear was a doctor in Rouen and a friend of Flaubert's. Louise lives upstairs with the kids. I'm downstairs with the dog—for the moment anyway.'

'Do you call that an estrangement?' Sylvie asked.

'I think we call it an arrangement.'

'You cook?' Bertholdt asked.

'Picard frozen dinners and Monoprix pizzas . . .'

'That's either tragic,' Sylvie said, 'or it's deplorable.'

'If it were true,' Max said, 'it might be both. I'm joking. I can do better than that for myself. And I have a lot of my meals upstairs with the troops.'

'So you're not banished.'

'Not banished, no. It's just . . . I'm not sure what. Something that happened.'

'A commendable disposition of space,' Bertholdt said. 'You'll probably stay married forever.'

'Like you and Gertrude,' Sylvie said.

'I think of it as time out,' Max said. 'A bit of space. *Distance*.'

'Only the distance between two floors,' Bertholdt said. 'That's a residence. It's a *domicile*.'

Max didn't say that Louise was on floor three while he was down at the level of the courtyard.

'Bertholdt has a wife in Berlin,' Sylvie said.

Bertholdt sighed and spread his hands in a gesture that said, 'Enough already.'

'And two sons,' Sylvie said.

There was unease now, and a brief silence. Max told them that, in the hierarchy of the Sorbonne Nouvelle, Louise ranked above him. 'She has leave from teaching at the moment to edit a new edition of *L'Éducation Sentimentale*.'

'Flaubert,' Bertholdt said.

'A very important work,' Sylvie said. There was a faint note of weariness—the well-brought-up schoolgirl acknowledging the classics.

'A long, dreary story of a man making mistakes,' Max said.

'One mistake,' Sylvie said, 'but it lasts—'

'A lifetime,' Max agreed.

'What is the mistake?' Bertholdt asked.

'Falling in love,' they said in unison.

'Of course,' Bertholdt said. 'What else in a nineteenth-century novel? And there are still new things to be said about the great Flaubert?'

'Always,' Max said.

Bertholdt shrugged. 'Scholars find new things to say about Goethe.'

Max explained, 'The old Rouen forebear's archives are being properly explored for the first time. There are letters that haven't been seen before. Some things in the biographies will have to be revised.'

'Scandals?'

'Nothing shocking. Flaubert was always very frank about his sex life.'

'Didn't he die of syphilis?' Sylvie said.

Max thought so but wasn't sure.

'A new edit of a major Flaubert,' she said. 'Your wife must be very distinguished.'

Max laughed. 'Too distinguished to walk the dog, yes.'

•

MAX HAD GONE AND SYLVIE and Bertholdt were getting ready for bed. They were cleaning their teeth, bumping into one another in the small tiled bathroom. 'I've heard of his wife,' Sylvie said. 'Professor Louise Simon-Jackson.'

'He seems pleased enough to be her husband even if he's banished downstairs.'

'Reflected glory, I guess.'

'Doesn't he have any of his own?'

'Academically? Some, yes. But he's nice, don't you think?'

Down in the streets the tumult continued, getting louder as midnight approached. It was as if they had turned Max loose into a storm.

She stood naked in front of the mirror, half-heartedly brushing her hair and looking at herself. 'Do you think I'm putting on weight?'

In a sighing tone he said, 'No, Sylvie.'

'I think I am.'

'Weigh yourself.'

'What do you mean, weigh myself?'

'*Weigh* yourself. Stand on the scales and read the dial. If it's higher than last time—'

'Oh get fucked, Bertholdt.' In her voice there was a hint of tears.

He sighed again, but went to her, still staring at herself in the mirror. He stood behind her and put his arms around her. 'Of course you're not putting on weight. Look at you.'

In the mirror he could see himself looking over her head, and his hands moving down towards her lower stomach, his fingers touching lightly all that was left of the pubic hair, shaved on either side, making a little Mohawk on the mound of Venus.

She put a hand behind her back. 'I could feel that happening,' she said.

She looked back over her shoulder and, still holding her from behind, he kissed her.

2.

WHY ONE

BUYS SHOES

JULIEN LEMONT, MAX'S CLOSEST COLLEAGUE, with whom he shared an office, was well known for exhibitions of eccentric behaviour. One in particular was a tantrum early in the academic year, at the first lecture to *agrégation* students. Julien, it was said, asked a question, something difficult, even abstruse, received an unsatisfactory answer, or no answer at all, and flew into a rage, berating the class as provincials unworthy of a great university, and then flung his notes across the room and stormed out. At his next scheduled meeting with the class he behaved as if the tantrum had not happened, and delivered a carefully prepared script (probably a fresh copy of the one previously thrown away) to a subdued and still shell-shocked class.

Perhaps the accounts Max heard of this were exaggerated, but something of the kind happened. The commonest explanation was that Julien believed he was despised by his colleagues, or at the very least was not valued by them, because he was himself a graduate from the provinces. To Max it was one of those matters that he put away under the general heading of 'peculiarly French' and therefore inexplicable.

In any case, Max liked Julien, found him amusing and clever company, and often had lunch with him. But he would have preferred not to share an office—something that never, or only very rarely, happened in anglophone universities, but was the rule here. Often, when he was interviewing a student and Julien was there working at his desk, Max would be sure the conversation was being listened to. There was something about Julien's breathing that signalled interest. The breath might be held, or let out in a sigh, sad or impatient; or now and then there might be something like a snort, quickly suppressed, disguised as a sneeze or a blowing of the nose, but indicating anything from amusement to outrage.

It was possible that Julien was not listening at all, was simply finding it difficult to concentrate on his own work. This sharing of spaces was part of the university's general lack of money. The state provided—but what it provided was never enough. The buildings, once you got beyond the grandeur that was for public show, were often shabby and run-down; and the determination of elderly conservationists to preserve, where possible, their original character and features made the problem worse. The amphitheatre where Max and Julien both did a large part of their teaching had been a theatre in which demonstration autopsies had been carried out in the Medical Faculty during the eighteenth century. The bust of some bewigged grand master of long ago stared down from behind the lecturer's back. The benches on which the students sat were so hard and badly designed it was impossible to be in them for more than an hour without pain. Echoes off hard surfaces made hearing difficult. Sometimes Max allowed himself to regret that Paris had been spared the Second World War pasting that London and Berlin had received.

Today Julien was not there, and Max was talking to a student who said she had come, not as a member of his class, but because she had found, in a long-ago issue of a literary magazine, *Poésies Vagabondages*, a long poem of his describing his experience as an outsider—in Paris for the first time, decidedly unhappy and yet also excited—'lit up', she said. She had found it 'thrilling', 'so vivid', and especially moving because she was herself an outsider—English (her name was Helen White) and 'mad'.

Max looked at her and decided the word 'mad' must be self-dramatisation, and best ignored. She appeared to be entirely sane; and, after all, she liked his poem so much.

'Yes I remember it well,' he said. 'I wrote it when I was first here as a postgraduate student. Before I'd met Louise . . . met my wife. It was one of my very few ventures into print as a poet.'

He felt himself smiling with a warmth he couldn't suppress. He'd been surprised and pleased with that poem—'From the dark place' it was called—and he remembered how writing it had more or less made up for miseries of loneliness, homesickness and physical discomfort. It was about France in winter, about Paris as an outsider sees it, romantic, rich in history and culture, but full of rain and darkness and uncertainty, inability to choose a place to eat, or decide which offered floor to sleep on. Those had been his disconsolate days, his days of depression and exaggeration, of acting the Existentialist, the Outsider, the Other.

'There was so much went into that poem,' he said, remembering encounters with sinister concierges and black-clad cops, gloomy rambles in the cemetery of Père Lachaise and the Luxembourg

Gardens. And then there had been all the excitements and discoveries of Art at the Beaubourg and the Jeu de Paume. He had somehow brought all this together with the obvious things, the clichés—croissants and millefeuilles, Jacques Brel and Édith Piaf, accordion music and black-and-white movies—finishing with the line, 'the Paris of Paris that's nobody's dream but your own'.

'It seems so long ago,' he said. 'I'm glad you found it, and that you liked it.'

'So now,' she said, 'I want to read more of your work.'

When he didn't respond she said, 'Your poetry—what you've written since.'

'Oh there's none,' he said. 'Nothing. The poetry bank's empty, I'm afraid. The cupboard's bare.'

She was shocked. 'But why?'

'Why? There's no why.' He was pleased, even flattered, that she liked what she'd found in that faraway place, but also irritated by the question. 'All I can tell you is, once I wrote poems and now I don't. I teach. My written work is for the academic journals.'

'Because you don't want to, is it, or because you can't?'

He took a deep breath, thinking the question was somewhat brutal. 'It's something that belongs to my past. Right now I'm afraid—' he patted the pile of examination scripts—'These won't be ignored.'

She said, 'Exam marking? I thought all that was finished by now.'

'These are second shots.'

It was something which French law required and which the Sorbonne did not always act on: that a student who failed an examination should be allowed to try a second time.

She half stood, while saying urgently, even darkly, 'No one writes a poem as good as that one and doesn't want to write another.'

She was speaking up for poetry now, its defender, as if he were standing in the way.

'One's life changes,' he said, feeling the weariness he heard in his own voice. 'One *moves on*—isn't that the cliché?'

Perhaps there was something in this that suggested he might after all want their conversation to continue. She heard it too and, very gently, sat down again. They stared at one another. The outer of several masks had been removed, his and hers. 'The person doesn't change,' she said. 'A poet is a poet . . .'

'. . . is a poet?' He looked up at her. 'You think? Well, maybe so. I'm still waiting.'

'For the Muse?'

He saw her more clearly now. She was not beautiful, and not ill-favoured, but distinct, noticeable, a well-defined face you might look at a second time because it gave you pleasure. Character, that was called; but there was something in the face that might be desperation. Rosa Dartle, he thought, remembering the wild woman, the only one with real character in *David Copperfield*. And then he remembered, or thought he did, that Rosa Dartle had described herself as 'mad'.

'A week or so ago,' Max said, 'I dreamed I'd written a poem. It was long enough to be published as a small book. Mostly my dreams are gone the next day, forgotten, but this one was so real it stayed with me. Even fully awake I was still not sure it wasn't true. I went hunting on my shelves for that little book just to be sure, even though I knew it didn't exist. I didn't remember it as a dream. I remembered it as a bit of my reality.'

This was something he had not told anyone. It had surprised him so much that the dream reality could hang on like that and assert itself so forcefully.

She was very still, listening, excited. 'That's either the next poem you will write,' she said, 'or it's the ghost of one you should have written and didn't.'

'Quite a powerful ghost,' he said. He was thinking he should not be having this conversation even as he began to ask what she'd meant—

He stopped himself, but she guessed what he was asking.

'When I said I was mad?'

'Yes.'

'I meant mad. Insane. Nuts.'

'I don't think I believe you,' he said. 'I'd rather not, if you don't mind.'

'I'm probably never entirely sane, but this is how I am as long as I take my medication. I've just had to accept it. Lithium. I don't like it. It dulls me, soothes me down, but it keeps me on the rails.'

Lithium. He remembered it was the medication that had kept the American poet Robert Lowell more or less normal. When he didn't take it, he tended to make scenes and smash things.

'I like to be brilliant,' she said, 'but it's better to be sane.'

He nodded, admiring. If that remark wasn't brilliant, there was at least something very clever about it.

'I've been diagnosed as bipolar,' she said.

'Here, or in England?'

'Ah.' She laughed, thought it was funny, and he saw that it was, as if sane in England might be mad in France, and vice versa.

'In England first,' she said. 'But the French health service is very good. They keep a watch on me and prescribe what I need. If I don't take the medication I have brilliant highs and then I can go right down—turn into one of those people you see out on the streets, shuffling around, sleeping rough, not coping. I was locked up in England—twice.' She shrugged and smiled. 'I have to be careful. Lithium's my necessary angel.'

He saw why she'd liked his poem. There had been something extreme about it, extravagant—something he was not capable of now. 'That poem of mine,' he said. 'It was full of exaggeration, you know. I never had to sleep rough . . .'

'It was full of feeling,' she said.

'I guess it was—yes. It was long ago.'

'You can't renounce it, Monsieur.'

'No, you're right. I can't. However . . .' Once again he put his hand on the pile of examination scripts.

'You want to get on with your work.'

'I don't want to, but I must.'

She stood, reached her right hand across the desk. Max shook it and said—not sure what he meant, but feeling grateful, and even hopeful—'You might be *my* necessary angel.'

She said, 'I hope so,' and darted away towards the door and through it, leaving him with the impression of a small animal scuttling away into the undergrowth.

•

IN THE SORBONNE NOUVELLE'S *Club des Enseignants* Sylvie Renard was listening to her colleagues talking about what was to be in the syllabus in the new academic year and beyond. There had been a meeting, and now the talk continued over coffee. She had not had a chance to speak to Max Jackson and he had left for something else before the meeting finished.

Sylvie knew her own preferences for what might be kept in, or scrapped from, the syllabus. But these were not only local decisions: they were also national, involving the Minister, and how the two, local and national, came together and reached an agreement was mysterious. She was not only junior (her rank was

Maître de Conférences), she was new, and had to feel her way with care. The Sorbonne, she knew, was Soviet in its bureaucracy and Ancien Régime in its hierarchy. Its absurdities and its grandeur, its importance and self-importance, were still new enough to be enjoyed from the sideline.

A lot of the meeting just over had been spent on the subject of internet protocol—whether colleagues should or should not be expected to answer email messages from students. Some thought yes, some no, some yes but only if the original message came with the correct form of address—'Monsieur or Madame le Professeur'—and ended with '*sentiments respectueux*' or a similar doffing of the cap and with the sender identifying themselves. No more responding to messages that began, 'Hey, dude!' and ended 'Jack'. This, after much debate, was what they had agreed.

Sylvie, amused, had been listening while at the same time her mind strayed elsewhere. Bertholdt had bought tickets for *Tosca* at the Opéra Bastille. Puccini would not have been her first choice but it was what was on offer, and she looked forward to it. But this put into her head the thought of clothes—and *shoes*. Bertholdt would take her first, or afterwards, to one of the chic bistrots nearby, probably Le Bofinger (said to have been President Mitterrand's favourite) or perhaps Les Grandes Marches, and she would want to look good. There was a pair of shoes she'd seen in a little shop on the rue du Cherche-Midi—fairy-tale shoes—she had even tried them on; and in the boutique two or three doors along there had been a lovely floaty scarf, midnight blue. Why had she not bought them—bought them both? What was the principle in operation that told her she should not be wasteful? What was 'waste' exactly? In this society at this time almost everything was waste—works of art, music, reading and talking about novels and poems, and, perhaps especially, opera. Everything we do, she thought, was at the expense of the future and of the poor. If you could afford something and thought it made your corner of the world a happier place . . . why hesitate?

It was not just predictions about global warming and a consequent sense of (she had heard the phrase a lot lately) 'species defeat' that promoted this feeling; it was (much worse) something she had read recently, not for the first time, but this time much more confidently and starkly expressed, about the universe—that it had a 'use-by' date; that the sun would cool and the earth would die. We were going to be swallowed by a black hole—or was it a black dwarf? Something like that. You might doubt these scientists. But when they could send a space vehicle on a ten-year journey that would bring it, after many millions of miles, as was happening right now, to a perfect rendezvous with a comet called 67P hurtling through space at 37,000 miles an hour and only a few miles across, and with the expectation of a landing there, it was reasonable to believe what they said. It was a better bet than the Church's 'sure and certain hope' of a life after death—because very soon the space vehicle would get there and send back images, and the science would be proved, or not—while the Church still waited for some word from the Beyond. Death—not just personal death but the Death of Everything—that, it now seemed, was the new Universal: 'Everything must go' as the sales said; and this was so much, so absolutely, more depressing than the knowledge that she and everyone she loved would die, and the confidence that nothing, no life after death, would follow. It was something the poets and philosophers of past times had not known, and which we of the twenty-first century had to accommodate. It was something Mozart and Beethoven had not known—nor Bizet, nor Lamartine, Balzac nor Victor Hugo. Racine had not known it, and neither had Shakespeare, Goethe, Dante, Cervantes. Not even

Tolstoy, in flight from his wife and dying in the railway station at Astapova—even he had been ignorant of this fact which she, Sylvie Renard, was burdened with as she thought about buying shoes. For Tolstoy everything would go on forever without him, while perhaps there might be a 'Heaven' for him to go to. But, Heaven or no Heaven, for Tolstoy there was no reason to suppose the world and the universe would not go right on as before.

These great figures of the past—they had never seen clouds from both sides, as Saul Bellow said in *Henderson the Rain King* (giving Joni Mitchell a line for her best song). They had never seen our planet from the outside, had never seen it as it was in reality, a beautiful blue-and-white orb; and they had certainly not known it had a use-by date. What would they have said? Take *that*, Racine!—let's see you wrap an Alexandrine or two around a cooling sun and a dying earth. And how about you, Shakespeare? 'Ripeness is all', eh? I'll say!

So Sylvie would go back and buy the shoes, if they were still there, and the *foulard* too; and maybe something else if she could find something and afford it. And then, arrayed like whoever it was in all his glory (and in some of his confidence), she would sip her cocktail at Le Bofinger or Les Grandes Marches, having drowned her senses in Puccini's romantic *Tosca*-tosh. Something nearer in time might have been better—Alban Berg's *Wozzeck*, for example. Something not entirely alien to the knowledge that the universe which began with a Big Bang will end with a Big Crash. But she would make do with *Tosca*, which was black enough, for all its sugar-coating.

Over coffee the conversation was rattling on but she had left it far behind. The subject had shifted from the meeting to things she knew nothing about. It was time to go.

At the door she met Max on his way back. She was so pleased she blushed, and then blushed because she was blushing. She repressed a momentary need to embrace him. She was too clearly on her way out to change direction and return. They were passing ships.

His face lit up in response to hers. 'Sylvie,' he said. 'You've had coffee already.'

'I have. And now I'm going to buy shoes.'

He laughed. 'A radical act!'

'It's because of global warming,' she said. 'And all the rest of it.'

'All the rest of it—of course. Couldn't be a better reason.'

'Bertholdt's taking me to *Tosca* at the Bastille next week. I have to be dressed for it.'

'*Tosca*. He's shot and she jumps off the battlements.'

Sylvie pretended not to know. 'Oh, Max—that's what's called a spoiler.'

He moved to pass her, but hesitated, touching her arm and breathing into her ear, 'Listen to the music and you won't care about the spoiler.'

•

MAX WAS SITTING UNDER THE awning of his local café, reading the latest brilliant opinion piece in the *Guardian Weekly*, in which it was argued that the corrections to the banking industry after the meltdown of 2008 had been only Band-Aids and aspirin, and that another, the same or worse, was on its way. It argued also that the middle class in the affluent West was not afflicted with anxiety about the poor, and in fact would be content to see the gap grow wider, not because they were vindictive or wished anyone ill, but because this reinforced their own sense of having succeeded in life. They were not, therefore, enticed by political programmes which promised welfare, greater equity and redistribution of wealth. The gap would have to get wider and the poor angrier, and therefore become a threat to peace and stability, before it would become politically significant.

At Max's feet under the table was his little bilingual dog, Skipper, who responded with equal excitement to the words 'a walk' or '*une promenade*', and whose name the waiters pronounced Skeep-aire.

Max moved on to more immediate international matters, skimmed here and there, and then put the paper aside, feeling he'd had enough, been more than adequately served by opinion pieces, the world's wisdom about the world's folly, which at this moment, and quite apart from high finance, was extreme—the Israelis squaring up to invade Gaza; Crimea becoming Russian again while separatists in the Ukraine were letting rockets loose into the skies; the war in Syria continuing bloody and relentless; Iraq breaking up into its ancient jigsaw, and the newest militant Islamists executing their opponents and hacking off the head of an American journalist, afterwards posting a video of the event on their website. And, in the United States, the first black president, who had come to power accompanied by high hopes and high-fives, was sounding and behaving like all the presidents before him. Negritude, it seemed, made no difference: to be America's president, whatever your skin colour, you had to be 'white' at heart.

So there was nothing to be done—neither taking up arms nor adopting the submissive posture would help. That was the big world of now: the world of 'Nothing-to-be-Done, alas!' Let the skies fall and let us run and tell the king!

Closer to home there was Monsieur Hollande, President of France, nominally a socialist and committed to defending the unions and shoring up the welfare state, but currently beset by women on three sides—Ségolène Royal, mother of his children, Valérie Trierweiler, for whom he had abandoned Ségolène, and who, now that he had abandoned her for the actress Julie Gayet, had written a tell-all book denouncing him. This—the book, not the behaviour—was deeply shocking. Even Marine Le Pen had said it was 'a dishonour to France'. It broke the unwritten law observed by the *nomenclatura* of the French Revolution no less than by the Ancien Régime that the sex lives of public figures were not to be treated as news. Nonetheless, scandal sells and the first edition of the Trierweiler book was gone already. When Max had visited his bookshop in search of a new novel by Martin Amis, just reviewed in *The Guardian*, he saw in the window a notice that said the bookseller was 'Truly sorry' that the Trierweiler book was sold out, but that he *did* have the works of 'BALZAC, DUMAS, MAUPASSANT, etc.'.

The waiters swooped here and there, and sometimes stood briefly at ease, their eyes moving as their bodies had done a moment before. They knew Skeep-aire, and tolerated him, sometimes feeding him titbits, a slice of salami or a corner of a croissant left on a plate. Not really hungry, Skipper snapped briskly at the donations, wagged his tail twice without getting up, returned his chin to rest on his front paws and closed his eyes.

The customers at tables arranged in cramped rows looked out towards the street and the square with its grand church, as if something were happening out there that must be, if not watched, at least regularly checked on. They were for the most part not the afternoon crowd and the tourists, who had time to spare and space for cake. Like Max, these were having breakfast. Those in the biggest hurry took it quickly and cheaply at the counter—usually just a small black coffee and a croissant; sometimes only the coffee. Max had *café au lait* and a croissant, with a bread roll and jam. He awarded himself breakfast here on days when there was time, and read a newspaper, English or French.

He thought of young English Helen, who had come to his office and had talked so enthusiastically about his poem of long ago. Now she had written him a letter, to his home address—he didn't know how or where she'd got that. From the faculty office he supposed, but it bothered him. She had begun in French and then drifted homeward, predominantly English but also Franglais, with deliberate comic effect. It had been delivered only this morning and he had skimmed it, intending to reread it here, over breakfast. But he didn't have it after all—he must have left it in the apartment, if he hadn't dropped it somewhere in the street.

She had told him about the teachings of Gurdjieff and how they helped her order her life—'Not life without lithium,' she said, 'but *in addition*: Gurdjieff as add-on; Gurdjieff as additive.' And now she wanted to tell him of her discovery that the New Zealand writer Katherine Mansfield had also been a follower of this great teacher, and had died at his Institute for the Harmonious Development of Man at Fontainebleau-Avon, just outside Paris. Helen was proposing that, with lectures now finished, he and she should go there together. It was a nice little village and there was a mini-tour that might show them the *prieuré* where Gurdjieff had taught, and Mansfield had listened and had watched the dances performed by the devotees. Perhaps this was something that might figure in a poem, when he went back to writing, 'as I know you will; as I know you must!'

Max made an effort to remember Helen's face. She was very persistent about his poetry and that was nice—irritating, but not unwelcome. He entertained himself by thinking of her as a Muse. He asked himself what he knew about Mansfield and could remember only stories about children in Wellington, and one about a man who drowned a fly in ink as a way of assuaging grief at the death of his son in the Great War. That subject again—

that war. How pressing it was at this moment (in these years!) of centenary commemoration.

•

LOUISE, RETURNING FROM WALKING THE children—Jean-Claude to the Métro at Saint-Sulpice, Juliette to her summer school in the rue Madame—decided she would call in at the downstairs apartment to check on Max. Some days he had breakfast in his kitchen, others upstairs with her and the children; and then there were times—this was new—when he took Skipper and had breakfast in the café on the Place Saint-Sulpice. This must be one of those mornings, because the door was locked, and when she let herself in Skipper did not greet her.

She wandered about, looking for signs, though of what? Max's bed was made and the flat seemed tidy. Louise had been working hard in recent weeks and was aware she had not paid him much attention. She wondered how he would spend his days, now that lectures were over and she was taking the children on holiday without him.

She breathed in the faint aroma of Max and felt a brief glow of affection, a sadness that she had, in effect, dismissed him downstairs. But she had been finding his presence, when she was working, distracting—no less so when they were getting on well than when they were not. There was the temptation always to tell him her latest discovery, or her latest theory about what it might mean. Either war or peace between them, it all amounted to time, and there was a publisher's deadline.

She drifted into the kitchen, looking in cupboards and drawers and in the fridge. There were no dishes in the sink, so he was at the café for breakfast. There was no bread, and not much food in the fridge. Maybe he intended to eat upstairs tonight—if so he hadn't warned her. Gina, her *femme de ménage*, would not be ready to provide, and would complain. Louise pulled her cell phone from a pocket and tapped in his number, then changed her mind, and switched it off. They had been seeing less of him lately. He was probably going to eat out with Julien Lemont who was for the time being also without a wife.

In the bedroom she pulled back the cover. His pyjamas under the pillow didn't appear to have been ironed, but they were folded. She sniffed his sheets, and then asked herself, because it had been done on an impulse, whether it had been to check on his hygiene or his fidelity. She was not sure, and decided it was both—curiosity really, and why not?—but she was careful putting the bedcovers back so there was no sign of what she'd done.

In the sitting room she looked over the table, with papers and examination scripts stacked in almost orderly piles at one end, and at the other the space, left clear, where he ate his meals. There was a notebook open and a full page of his handwriting. He still did first drafts by hand and dated the page, and she saw this one was today's date. He must have been up early writing. She read a few sentences, and then had to read it all. It was elegant, concise. It sounded as if it might be a conclusion, summing up and rounding off with a comparison of his two subjects, Doris Lessing such an effortless writer, V.S. Naipaul so effortful—the pleasure and the pain felt in every sentence of the one and the other; and yet neither, he went on, was 'better'.

Louise did not feel she should turn the page and read more. She had not even touched the notebook, had crouched over it. But she was impressed by what she'd read. That was Max: not a literary theorist at all—theory didn't interest him—but a critic, lucid and persuasive, who could give you the feel of the book he was writing about.

Also on the table she now saw there was a single letter, two pages, possibly more, lying on top of the pile as if it had just been read. She kept her distance. Letters were even more private than first drafts. She thought of herself as a woman of honour, well brought up in a family of some consequence in France (and not merely, or only, in banking and munitions); and one of the things impressed upon her by her father, who received many important letters, was that a person of honour did not read another's correspondence unless invited to. But it was so unusual these days to see a real letter on notepaper and sent by post, when most communication was by email or text, that she couldn't resist staring at it and wondering about it. She took in the signing-off at a glance, shied away from it guiltily, and then stopped to think about what she'd read.

It was signed '*Je t'embrasse*' and then 'Helen (White)'. That was odd. The '*Je t'embrasse*' was intimate, while putting the surname in brackets, as if he might not be sure which 'Helen' was embracing him, suggested the contrary.

She looked again, reasoning with the ghost of her father. Max had left the letter open on the table—had not attempted to hide it. That was no excuse, the ghost told her: she did not have permission.

But what if Max was having an affair with this 'Helen (White)' who ended her letter with an embrace?

She was reflecting that to still be dominated, in what was her near middle-age, by the fear of displeasing her long-dead papa was ridiculous, when she heard Skipper scratching at the door, and the rattle of keys.

'Louise,' Max said, startled—and then, 'Morning, stranger,' and kissed her on both cheeks. It felt pleasantly affectionate, but more distant than she might have liked, as if they were acquaintances greeting one another in the street. Skipper, released from his leash, jumped up to greet her, wholehearted—she liked that. Satisfied with a pat and having his ears ruffled, he went to his water dish in the kitchen and lapped noisily.

Max had a baguette under one arm and carrier bags from which he unloaded a wedge of cheese, a salami sausage, tomatoes, a lettuce, two peaches.

Louise said, 'I'm glad you're providing for yourself. The cupboard looks pretty bare.'

'Checking up on me are you?' he said in a tone that indicated he didn't mind—might even be glad. They were out of the kitchen now and he picked up the letter, casually, and added it, face down, to the pile at the other end of the table.

'A real letter,' she said. 'From the postman. You don't see that very often.'

For just a moment he looked at her, as if he might have been wondering what she meant, whether she was telling him something. And then: 'I used to get letters like that from my sister—with those nice New Zealand stamps that went into Jean-Claude's collection.' There was a pause before he said, 'We should take Johnny and Julie to New Zealand.'

We. She wondered, Did he mean that? Was he hoping they might be 'we' again? She moved towards the door. 'You've been out for breakfast.'

'And to walk Skipper.'

Skipper's ears went up at the sound of his name and the magic word. He opened his mouth wide and seemed to smile, panting, his tongue lolling sideways. 'Tell *me*,' he seemed to say, with a faint wag of the tail.

'How's Flaubert treating you?' He pronounced it as it would be if it were English—Floe-Bert—a meaningless joke between them, repeated so often it passed unnoticed.

'I think the end's in sight. But annotations—they take so much time.'

'Bored?'

'Not bored—no, not at all. Weary.'

'It's a long, slow book.'

'It's not all that long, Maximus, but slow—yes. I noticed on my latest run-through that Frédéric sees Madame Arnoux on the paddle-steamer on just about the first page and they reach the point where they can admit to being in love on page two hundred and seventy. Then there's another hundred before she's ready to "give herself to him", as they say . . .'

'Yes,' he said. 'That's slow.'

'It's the politics I'm focusing on at the moment—especially when it turns into civil unrest and shooting in the streets.'

'1848?'

'Exactly.'

'Is it true Flaubert died of the pox?'

'He contracted syphilis in 1850,' she said.

'But it wasn't what killed him?'

'He died of a stroke—though I don't suppose having the pox, as you call it, helped. Why?'

'It came up in conversation the other night.'

'With?' But he didn't hear—or chose not to answer.

'Right, well . . .' She felt strangely crushed by that little silence; shut out by it. 'Time to get back,' she said.

He came closer, close enough to put his hands on her upper arms, and then slide them down to her hips on either side. There was something about his ease at that moment, a confident assertion of masculinity that she hadn't seen in him in many months.

She laughed. 'What are you doing?'

'I'm embracing my wife.'

'Thank you.' And she kissed him briefly. She remembered the letter with its '*Je t'embrasse*', and said, 'Are you in love with someone?'

The question surprised her as much as it surprised him, and she could see he didn't have a ready answer. He moved back a couple of steps and looked at her, turned away as if displeased and then turned back to face her. 'Possibly. Yes, something like that.'

'Good for you,' she said, but it was not what she felt as she headed for the door. She went out, closing it carefully, not wanting to seem to be 'storming out'.

3.

FAMILY

AND FRIENDS

MAX WAS EATING ALONE IN a pizza and pasta place, Il Palazzo, on the Boulevard Saint-Michel just up from the rue Racine. He was at a single table right on the pavement, facing out. The boulevard sloped away to his left, and down there on the Île de la Cité the face of Police Headquarters, known as 'Trente-Six', seemed to be swathed in bandages, with some kind of advertisement or public notice projected onto it. Beside his plate of *melanzane parmigiana* and his glass of Chianti he had the new Martin Amis novel, *The Zone of Interest*, and was reading and rereading its opening section, which began, 'I was no stranger to the flash of lightning, I was no stranger to the thunderbolt' and ended a page later, 'Something happened at first sight. Lightning, thunder, cloudburst, sunshine, rainbow—the meteorology of first sight.'

Of course the young Amis who, like the young Dumas, was forever young to distinguish him from his father the late Kingsley, would probably take hefty blows for this novel, 'because' it was about the Holocaust and was set in Auschwitz, too serious a subject (in fact a defining moral marker of the century just past) to be appropriate, or even proper, for fiction, especially fiction that had comic intent. But would the 'because' be much more than an excuse for the beating? When did a beating ever not have a 'because'; and when did a new book by 'young' Amis not receive one? It was something about the style of the man, and his refusal to hide the light of his genius under a bushel of green tea. As some writers emanated moral merit, Amis put talent on display. This was what a study of the literary life taught; and Max, to keep it in mind, and to explain the Amis phenomenon, had kept a review of a collection of Amis essays, which he transferred from book to book as each new one appeared. It was by someone called Geoff Dyer, a younger writer (younger than Amis) and it began, 'Something strange was going on. I realized a third of the way through this box of Amis all-sorts, I was reading these pieces with the intention of giving him a good trimming—even though I'd been gulping them down with unquenchable relish. Such a reaction is not, I suspect, untypical. Amis's prose seems to invite competitive disparagement as the appropriate register of admiration.'

Competitive. Well, at least Geoff had stopped himself in time, which he hadn't always done; and Max kept the clipping as an explanation of why Amis, often acknowledged as the major talent of his generation, had only once been shortlisted, and had never won, the Booker Prize, that major distraction and perennial cause of discord and confusion in the anglophone world of books.

Max stuffed the tattered reminder back into the end pages of the novel and allowed himself to think instead about 'the meteorology of first sight'—the *coup de foudre*, as the French called it, the same thunderclap that had convinced Flaubert's character Frédéric Moreau, at the age of eighteen, that he was in love with Madame Arnoux, a conviction that would dog him for a lifetime and make all his biggest decisions mistakes. Max was not eighteen and not French; he had, or believed he had, a sense of irony and an ability to criticise, even to mock, himself. But that meteorology, where Amis had chosen to begin his new novel, interested him now because it was what he thought he had experienced with Sylvie Renard. She was the invader who had mysteriously moved in and taken possession of the house of his mind; and for Max the point of going after a new Amis book was to take it back again—part of it anyway. Amis's genius was large in language, and it was the English language that Max missed especially. He was competent in French, and pleased with himself that he was. But he knew there were very subtle registers of taste, vocabulary, grammar which he possessed in his mother tongue and not in French.

More simply, he missed English as you miss the landscape of home. Amis, by bringing him home to the language, would help to take his mind off Sylvie; so it was an irony and an inconvenience that his new novel should begin with this little disquisition on love at first sight.

He had finished his *melanzane* and was thinking about *crème brûlée* when Sylvie's Bertholdt Volker came into sight. Another reminder! Fate was against him. The German was carrying a briefcase and he was frowning. It was the kind of frown a man trying to make sense of Strindberg's *The Ghost Sonata* (or perhaps a man living with quicksilver Sylvie?) might be expected to wear.

He was not walking briskly, as Max, having talked to him on

midsummer's night, would have expected. Not dragging his feet either, but there was something *trudging* about his step, as if the slight rise of the boulevard away from the river were steeper than it was in fact. He had his eyes fixed ahead, into the distance and on nothing, so had not seen Max, who decided he would not call out to him. 'I'll let this one pass,' said Max, entertaining himself. But now, still looking ahead, the German veered towards him and held out his hand.

So Max had been seen somehow, peripherally. It had a strange effect, the hand held there, the eyes still seeming to look left in the direction he'd been going. Max shook it. It was a large hand, obscurely intimidating to Max, whose hands were small.

And now, as Bertholdt did look at him, Max recognised a slight upward shift in the German's mood. Something pleased him. Max thought he knew what it was. Bertholdt was probably asking himself why, in Paris, which must have more eating places than any city in the world, one would choose to eat here—and so conspicuously, stuck out on the pavement as if inviting anyone who knew you to take note? Inwardly, Max made the kind of joke Bertholdt might be making. Was the management paying him to eat there?

Max felt in quick succession embarrassed, defensive, annoyed; then amused and finally indifferent. The truth was he liked the *melanzane* and the glass of Chianti very much. It was close to the Sorbonne Nouvelle and had become, not a ritual, but an irregular, simple pleasure.

'Please—join me.' He signalled to the chair on the other side of his table.

'*Danke*,' Bertholdt said, and eased himself into it, sighing like an inflatable going down, and lowering his briefcase carefully to the pavement.

Would he order something to eat? Or a drink?

Bertholdt shook his head. Thank you, no. He would a moment rest. It had been an early start and a long day.

They exchanged remarks about the weather, while Max wondered if Bertholdt was unwell and decided probably he was not. Tired, bored perhaps, but strong as an ox. It was just that the momentary pleasure of his thought about Max's choice (if he'd had such a thought) was quickly gone.

Bertholdt said, 'Sylvie has been texting me about today's faculty meeting.'

Max said in English, 'It was a bit fraught, actually.'

'Fraught.' Bertholdt had not understood. '*Bitte?*'

So his English, which Sylvie had said was better than his French, had its limits, and Max, momentarily competitive, was not sorry. He reverted to French, saying that nerves were frayed at this time of year, and academics were typically an argumentative lot.

'There was something about who gets the chairs and who has to stand if there are not enough.'

Max nodded. 'Yes there are protocols and precedents. Upset her, did it?'

'Not too much. I think she was amused—finally.'

'She's new to the Sorbonne.'

Bertholdt didn't reply. He was looking at Max. Was he expecting an explanation—perhaps an apology? What was he—her lawyer? Her father?

Max said, 'To some of us from anglophone countries it's what we think of as "European".'

Bertholdt fixed him with a pale northern stare. 'European? European *what?*'

'Regimentation,' Max said. 'A tendency, you know?'

'I thought England was the home of the class system.'

'True. But this might be something subtly different. Napoleonic?

Prussian, perhaps. Military? I have to say it's new to me. Allocation of chairs according to seniority . . .'

Bertholdt shrugged, loosened his collar. 'You are right, Professor. It is today very warm.'

Max was glad to be right, and not unwilling to be 'Professor'; but had he said anything about the heat? Perhaps he had. There was an empty glass on his side of the table. He filled it and pushed it across.

Bertholdt wiped the back of his neck with a handkerchief and said nothing. His eyes were half closed. He was perhaps thinking about regimentation, and class, and how they differed, and did they? Or thinking nothing of the kind.

Max filled his own glass and drank. He noticed that the street lights had come on and the sky was beginning to darken.

Struggling to make conversation he said, 'I love eating out in these long evenings. Eating and reading. I heard someone on France Inter saying you shouldn't do it. You should enjoy one pleasure and then the other, not both at once.'

Bertholdt nodded slightly. He said nothing, and Max went on. 'Of course as it gets darker . . .'

'Sylvie is the reader in our household,' Bertholdt said.

'I can imagine.'

'And your book?' enquired Herr Volker, looking at Max's copy of *The Zone of Interest*, still open on the table.

'Martin Amis's latest,' Max said. And then, 'A novel.' And then, and with no conscious motive, but a dim feeling there might be an unconscious one, 'It's about the Holocaust.'

'The Holocaust.' Bertholdt repeated it. His voice was deep, rumbling, indistinct but not undistinguished. 'I must let you get on with that.'

'Set in Auschwitz.'

'Auschwitz, my God!' He stood and picked up the briefcase.

'Amis writes so well.' Max heard himself say this and thought it probably sounded to the German at least puzzling, possibly ridiculous.

Bertholdt shook his hand. 'Goodnight, Herr Professor.' He offered a creaky smile. 'Auschwitz . . . I wish you sweet dreams.'

Max watched Sylvie Renard's friend, partner, lover, whatever he was—ploughman, perhaps—'homeward plod his weary way'— up the darkening boulevard.

•

HELEN WHITE WAS SITTING ON the grass with her back against a tree just inside the iron gates of the Luxembourg Gardens, eating an ice cream she had bought from the vendor's cart out there on the street, and dreaming of home. Like (she thought) 'Drake was in his hammock and a thousand miles away, slung a'tween the round-shot in Nombre Dios Bay, and dreaming all the time of Plymouth Hoe.'

Nombre de Dios must be name of God. Funny, she'd never thought of that. When she'd sung it as a child she'd thought it had something to do with number. *Nombre de Dios.* Drake had God's number. But home for her had not been Plymouth Hoe and was not at this moment a thousand miles away. It had been in the not very wild wilds of Wiltshire—or would you call it the West Country? Somewhere in between, perhaps. And then Oxford, where her mother had been a paediatrician at the Radcliffe and her father a Fellow of St John's. And now she supposed it must be Norfolk, where the parents lived, semi-retired, but still both professionally busy, in a beautiful old mill-house with wooden beams inside and white weatherboards out, and the millstream running by under willows, and with a wood, or perhaps it was a spinney or copse, of poplars at the back. (A spinney of poplars. A copse of poplars. She tried them both for sound and liked them equally.) She had gone to school in Oxford, and then to university there, and had flourished, she thought—everyone thought—until her mind became over-filled with poems, including one by Edward Thomas called 'Adlestrop'.

It was not just the poem that became an obsession but the word. Adlestrop. It represented Englishness, the country rail-stop in late June surrounded by willows in full leaf, with meadows and pasture and hay and a blackbird; and then, as in the Hitchcock movie, the just one bird became all the birds of Oxfordshire and Gloucestershire—a congregation of polluters of silence, which was what birds were if you cared about it, if your ears were sensitive. And if you said the word Adlestrop to yourself too often the birds got more confused and the scene mistier until everything was lost and there was just ADLESTROP, too many consonants fighting for the light—sinister, secret, dangerous, and perhaps hinting at something you did not want to know, ever . . .

Time to change the subject. So she went in her head to Gerard Manley Hopkins, always a comfort: 'Margaret, are you grieving, Over Goldengrove unleaving?' Gerry Hopkins, the unhappy priest of so long ago, who 'caught this morning morning's minion' and wrote about the cutting down of the Binsey poplars at Oxford, which had, since his time, grown again and could be seen on the walk across the Port Meadow from Southmoor Road to a pub called The Trout . . .

Oxford, where she had encountered the philosopher Roger Scruton with his idea that there were two kinds of metaphysics, descriptive and revisionary, and she had tried, in an essay for her tutor at St Anne's, to apply the same distinction to poetry, making

Keats the 'descriptive' poet and Blake the 'revisionary'. Blake, not Drake: not the Ache who was in his hammock and a thousand miles away, but William Blake in his London garden, naked with Mrs Blake, pretending to be Adam and Eve. Two of them, Mr and Mrs. The Naked Blakes. Aching like Drake.

Baking: she was baking in the sun and the ice cream was done. She would have liked another but lay on her back listening to the traffic, wheeled and footed, whirring wheels and clacking heels; and she looked through the trees at the sky, like the sky at Adlestrop, with small white cloudlets, floating. I could be happy there, she thought. It was better to be Keats than Blake, Keats than Shelley, Kelly than Sheets. And when was it she had first encountered that book by Derrida and the sentence that had taken hold of her, demanding she understand it though she didn't and couldn't, and yet she had wrestled with it? She said it over: 'We are dispossessed of the longed-for presence in the gesture of language by which we attempt to seize it.' Her boyfriend in Oxford had said this was a description of a failed rugby tackle. His name was Hugh Pennington and he came to Oxford from Rugby, and played it. He was reading science, biochemistry, and played the violin too.

Hugh had tried to keep her there in Oxford but Derrida had won, had brought her to Paris, though he was already dead, had been dead ten years. In fact on 8 October, only a few months away, it would be a decade exactly. She had thought she would be nearer to his mind, the French mind, if she put herself inside the French language, but perhaps she should have taken his Algerian childhood into account and gone there. Would that have helped, nothing would have helped, Derrida was like his name, or a nursery rhyme, something you just had to struggle with and make the best of, like the refrain of a song by Shakespeare, da derri-*da* down dilly, and da derri-*da*.

Thinking this in a kind of silent singalong she drifted asleep for a few minutes and dreamed she was in a room with high sash windows wide open and white curtains billowing in a breeze. Beyond was the green of trees and lawns and the mild thwack and knock of tennis. She was dressed all in white and so was Hugh, who was also Max Jackson; and perhaps she and Max had just made love because she was telling him he did not know what it was to feel shame. He said (and now it was definitely Max) this was nonsense, everyone knew Shame, Shame was everybody's friend, and she'd had an answer for that, perhaps about degrees of it, but as she woke she couldn't remember what it was, only that it was a good one, unanswerable . . .

What she needed now was to be conscious, in the Gurdjieff sense of consciousness, which included focus, finding her centre. Professor Jackson—Max, as she was allowed to call him—had agreed to come with her to Fontainebleau, where they would go on a small organised tour to the house and gardens that had been Gurdjieff's Institute for the Harmonious Development of Man. Max had sent her a nice little message in reply to her letter, agreeing to meet her at the Gare de Lyon.

No need for shame. She must be mindless, centred; must pass through the gateless gate and walk freely between heaven and earth. She must work towards Zen, towards enlightenment, towards Satori . . .

•

MAX WOKE AND CHECKED HIS watch: 3.25 a.m. and very dark. Small and changing fractures of light around the curtains; a car, its sound, no headlights flashing by because the gate was closed on the courtyard. And now a distant klaxon. Voices, his and hers, beyond the courtyard, but quite loud and echoing in the empty street—quarrelling, were they, or happy? It was hard to tell—and soon gone, leaving something like a moment of perfect silence. Paris could sleep sometimes, cat-nap, even in midsummer. From the next room in that silence came the small, familiar sounds Skipper made while sleeping in his basket—there!—a kind of quiet whine that meant he was dreaming. Did he dream in French or in English?

Max was remembering his childhood in New Zealand, and a girl, Christine Nixon, who had lived with her parents in one of a block of four flats just down the street from his parents' house. She was two or three years older than Max, blonde, blue-eyed, and he had thought her stunningly beautiful. Once he'd dreamed of kissing her in the windowless space where wood and coal for winter fires were stored under their house. He never had, then or later, exchanged a word with Christine. She was just *there*, a beautiful presence, seen in the street or the schoolyard, not noticing him, not knowing she was the source of a dream which remained with him, not sexual (he was too young for that), just intense, delicate, ravishing.

Not more than a year ago Raymond Parker, a former school friend, now a successful international businessman, had come through Paris, and had invited Max ('and your lady partner, if you have one currently') to dinner at his flash hotel, the Four Seasons on the rue George V between the Champs-Élysées and the Seine. This was before Max and Louise's upstairs-downstairs separation, but relations were uneasy; she had opted for something more to her taste and he had gone alone.

It was, Ray Parker reported, his first time in Paris and he was enjoying it. He had 'dropped in at the Louvre for a shufti at the Mona Lisa and so on'; he'd been 'up the Eiffel Tower and down the Seine', the latter on a *bateau mouche*; he'd stumbled into the

Musée d'Orsay and been 'pretty amazed'. Max responded in the way it seemed his friend required, confirming that, yes, these were the things to see, the places to go. It was an unpromising start. But then they'd begun to talk about 'old times', as you do with school friends you haven't seen in decades, and at once they were at ease, enjoying themselves, remembering, prompting one another. So it had emerged that Christine Nixon was Ray's cousin, something Max had not known.

Max told him that she had been a kind of *beau idéal* of his childhood; that he supposed he could say he'd been childishly in love with her.

Ray, a pleasant, generous realist with a big voice, enjoying his own affluence and glad it was possible to spread some of it around in this 'world-famous city', laughed heartily. Christine Nixon? Cousin Christine? She was a bitch. No other word would do. Bitch supreme. Totes bitch. Bitch with a very big B. He'd thought so even when they were kids. Fanatical anti-smoker now, gin-drinker, big-spender, tough on her kids, kept her husband on a very short leash. 'The only thing she loves is her dog,' Ray concluded. 'Another bitch.'

So that was her then! The subject changed and she was forgotten—until now, in the dark of Paris and his downstairs apartment, when Max woke remembering that childhood dream, which had been, he had thought, an early awakening to beauty with a very big B. But the shock of this 3.25 a.m. moment had been the recognition that Sylvie Renard, the Sylvie who had become an inexplicable midsummer obsession, was like a new incarnation of Christine Nixon.

Did they have anything in common? Or was this only some kind of transference of an intellectual idea, an ideal? Would anyone he fell in love with (had he 'fallen in love'?) have taken on the form and colour, the aura, the romantic ambience of Christine Nixon, so delicately dreamed among the stacks of cut wood and the sacks of coal? Was she only his 'necessary angel', as Helen White's was lithium?

•

LOUISE HAD SETTLED TO HER work, anxious that it was moving too slowly and not wanting interruptions, but when the phone rang she answered it. The message, which came from a rather frosty second cousin, was that her uncle Henri, her late father's brother, had died aged ninety-one.

'I apologise for being the bearer of sad tidings,' the cousin said.

Louise said, 'One needs to know of course. Thank you for telling me.' And after a pause, 'The funeral . . .'

Details were yet to be decided upon. She would be informed, he said, and she thanked him again.

'Au revoir, Madame,' he said.

'Au revoir, Monsieur.' *Distant* cousins.

Why had she picked up the phone? She reproached herself—too easily distracted, a willing victim, an easy lay, *une femme facile*.

There were anxieties connected with the work. Flaubert was not the most fashionable of the French classics at the moment. If, as the theorists liked to say these days, 'the author is dead' and the work comes into existence only at the moment of being read, Flaubert was more 'dead' than in the days when Louise was young and had been able to create a small sensation in the classroom by announcing that one of her forebears had been his friend and his doctor. Because Flaubert was an accepted 'classic' of French literature he would not vanish from the canon and the syllabus, and there would always be a place for the work she was presently doing. But feminism had not been kind to him, just as he had not been kind to his best-known female character, Emma Bovary. All his thought, all his care, had gone into the work itself, into the pursuit of what he called '*le mot juste*'—the perfectly chosen word, preferably one that had no exact synonym and which he would fix in place in perfect aural and lexical harmony with the words that came before and after. Flaubert would spend hours, sometimes days, getting a single sentence, even a single phrase, perfect. So much concern for the word meant there was little left for the character; and Louise's female colleagues sometimes made her feel she was a traitor to her sex, giving too much time, space and energy to a man who, if he was not a misogynist, was at least antipathetic to the cause of women.

Floe-Bert: that was Max's English (or anglophone, as he would prefer) way of putting the great Frenchman, 'the Big Frog', in his place. Was that the point? Or was there no point at all? Was it 'just a joke'—the sort of anarchic playfulness she tried to engage in when he seemed to require it, but which did not come naturally to her and which she found—what? Inappropriate, unbecoming, even childish were some of the words she'd used when they quarrelled. She thought of other words now—unsuitable, un-French. It was a kind of Anglo behaviour that didn't feel right to her.

As she traversed these old grounds she found herself straightening the works on the wall—and then simply touching, fondly, the one they called 'the picture'—the only one that was firmly in place, not screwed down but with two hooks rather than one so it was always horizontal. Other works, knocked off-centre by the feather duster of Gina, might need straightening. Gina, Italian and Catholic, seemed to dislike the nudes, particularly the males. It was a joke in the family that after Gina had been at work you had to straighten the pictures.

Louise touched the light modern frame of 'the picture'. It was not one the artist himself would have chosen. In fact it was thought he had never framed the painting. Although it was a small work, Louise was sure he would have wanted something a little more solid and ornate. But this was how it had come to them and she was content with that. Of all the many lovely things they owned this was by far the most valuable, the one looked at most often and thought about most. It sang to her. It was what had seemed to require their high-quality burglar alarm. Not that it had been authenticated by experts. But there was no need for that. Its origin, and its passage down the generations of her family, was fully recorded, in letters and in wills.

From time to time she had thought of selling it—but not seriously. She loved 'the picture', and she loved owning it—and how could the two be separated? At the time when she and Max had been described as a brilliant couple, an example of Anglo–French *entente cordiale*, in their days of soirées and dinner parties here in the generous space of the third-floor apartment, it had shone under its wall light, not a large work but one that dominated the room— the colours, the overhanging summer greens of the woodland, the sinister shadow and mysterious splash of orange over the water of the pool, all unmistakable to the cognoscenti. Even in the family it went without its proper name, like one of those stories in ancient myth in which a name, though known, must not be spoken for fear of bad consequences. But the name was an open secret, and it seemed its value could only increase. One became richer simply by owning it: nothing more was required.

It was the telephone call that had taken her at once to the picture, to marvel at it, feeling a special communion with it, because it was her uncle Henri who had claimed, on the death of Louise's father, that this family heirloom should pass to him. Her grandfather had left it to her father, Claude, the younger of his two sons, and the modest family château to Henri, the older; and as the years had gone by the one had increased in perceived or anticipated value while the other had declined. To own the château cost money, especially in winter, when heating it had become so expensive that Henri had given up trying, and kept it only for family holidays in summer. With Claude's death, Henri had argued through his lawyers that this had not been foreseen by their father and it was not what he would have wanted. The painting and the château should both have been shared. But the court had ruled that the château was the true principal *patrimoine*, and it was correct that it had gone to the older son. Sometimes, though not often, it could be bad luck to be the older son; but in these matters French law allowed no exceptions.

Henri had not forgiven Louise for her successful defence of her grandfather's will, which meant that Claude's right to leave the painting solely to her could not be challenged, while he, on the other hand, could not enforce that the cost of keeping up the château be shared. Now there would have to be a funeral that would bring the family together for the Mass, and at the Montparnasse cemetery, where she assumed Uncle Henri would be interred in the family mausoleum alongside (or on top of—she was not sure how things were managed) the brother who had been his not altogether loving rival. And, what would make it all more fraught, there was said to be a war between Henri's second wife, now his widow, and his two daughters by his first. It was over money of course, a situation Flaubert would have dealt with exquisitely.

Louise pressed in the security-code numbers and took the lift down, wishing the concierge, Monsieur Ferney, good morning as she passed his lodge. This little excursion too, was against her own rule. She had promised herself that she would keep office hours.

She had Gina as daytime *femme de ménage* to do the shopping, run errands, pick the children up from their schools, and prepare a meal for the family, so no need for Louise to stir outdoors. But the news of Uncle Henri's death had let loose thoughts that could not be lightly shrugged off there at her desk. She would walk a few blocks and have a coffee somewhere.

So she strolled along the rue Bonaparte and browsed in the bookshop on the corner, La Procure. There in the window was Valérie Trierweiler's book, with its heavily ironic title, *Thank You for That Moment*—a kick in the teeth for the President of the Republic, François Hollande. Such an angry woman, who had said her rival in love, Julie Gayet, should be hung by the ankles (like the body of Mussolini's mistress, Clara Petacci) from a tree in the grounds of the Department for the Environment where Ségolène Royal, her other rival, was the minister. Louise liked what Marine Le Pen had said about the book—that it dishonoured France.

Louise had voted for Madame Le Pen in the presidential election —another cause (one of the worst) of discord between herself and Max. They might have voted together for the socialist Ségolène Royal; but the party had chosen Ségolène's former husband, lover, whatever—father of her children—the ineffectual Hollande as its candidate. Louise felt cheated, and that Ségolène had been cheated; it was time for a first female president of France, and there had been a good one on offer—capable, eloquent, intelligent, presentable. Louise would not vote for Hollande; and she would not vote for Nicolas Sarkozy, with his tall Italian glamour-wife and his platform shoes. So she had voted for Marine Le Pen.

Max was outraged, accused her of reverting to the pattern of her benighted Gaullist family; and it was not untrue that it had given her a small thrill to know that, for the first time since she began voting, this was one her father would not have been displeased by.

There were things she liked about Madame Le Pen, and others (mostly inherited from Le Pen senior) that caused anxiety. But it had been a vote for a woman by a woman, and she would not apologise for it—especially now that Hollande seemed in public unable to act decisively, and in private the victim of his own mistaken choices.

The arguments over that election spread in all directions. They were a blur now, and were only part of a bigger picture of discord; but at the end Max was down and she was up—literally at least, but perhaps in spirit too. Her 'English' husband was in his place, downstairs, and she was in hers.

She permitted herself to wonder what he was doing now that classes were over. He seemed determined that this summer he would finish the little book he was writing on the two novelists and Nobel Prize winners, V.S. Naipaul and Doris Lessing; and the draft page she'd read looked like a conclusion—though she knew he wrote his books in a strange order. He was perfectly capable of writing the end before he had reached it.

But it was no use expecting to know what he was up to if they weren't sharing the same space, the same breakfast table, the same bed. And yes, it was better that way. As things stood, she was sure it was better for them both.

•

MAX'S SISTER JENNY HAD EMAILED. It was a long message—for her, very long. There had been an election in New Zealand and Labour, which she supported, had been beaten. So, a triumph, she said, for 'Prime Minister Dead-eyes', and that would mean more of the same . . . dismantling the . . . privatising the . . . pandering to the . . .

Jenny was ranting now; and in any case he knew most of this from the New Zealand papers he skimmed online. He was skimming her message now, letting his mind drift, his attention half switched to *Télématin*. Islamist militants had beheaded a French tourist and posted the video on Facebook. In New York at the United Nations, François Hollande, looking jet-lagged and harassed, had denounced this 'brutal and cowardly act', and in Nice (a switch on the television from New York to a seafront scene with palms), where the murdered tourist came from, the mayor declared himself heartbroken.

And now here was Nicolas Sarkozy, back from the dead, saying he'd done a lot of thinking and had learned a lot since his election defeat two and a half years ago . . .

Max, finishing his breakfast, poured himself more coffee, broke in two the last piece of the fresh, crusty baguette he had bought this morning, added butter and gave a corner to Skipper, thinking about that name: Sarkozy. He imagined the white-coated one he thought of as Dr Death, solemn, 'I'm sorry to have to tell you, Monsieur, but the tests are unambiguous. Your *Sarkozy* is inoperable. I would say you have three months. Six at most. I'm sorry.'

Now the Indian Prime Minister, Narendra Modi, was on the screen. An Indian satellite had travelled almost a year and was now in position alongside Mars, ready to go into orbit; and this had cost, the prime minister was pointing out, less than it had cost Hollywood to make the space movie *Gravity*.

In Scotland the referendum had gone in favour of remaining in the Union, and a mike in New York had picked up UK Prime Minister David Cameron telling someone that the Queen had purred into the phone when he had called about it.

In East Africa the Ebola crisis was worsening and Médecins Sans Frontières were warning—

Max found the remote and clicked it off. It interested him, all this stuff, but there was some part of him that resisted, knowing he should not allow his mind to be blown away, out over vast tracts of 'history as it was happening', but should be pulled in, focused on where his reading of Naipaul and Lessing had taken him yesterday. Ideas had come to him in the night, but would he remember them? Would they be used?

As he looked over the scribbled thoughts, which now barely made sense, he remembered the dream he'd had before or after—two men, both of them the British prime minister, one in a darkish blue, heavily textured suit, tweed perhaps, with darker (but still blue) stripes or bands. Max had told this Cameron how much he admired it, and then felt uneasy that he'd said nothing to the other about what *he* was wearing, which was perfectly satisfactory but not in any way special. Both Camerons had remarked pleasantly on his corduroy jacket, but he had known this was only politeness. They had no opinion about his jacket.

His cell phone rang. Louise wanted him to pick up Jean-Claude from his friend's house this afternoon. Would he do that?

Yes, he would, of course. How was she—were they?

They were fine, 'full of beans and a box of birds' she said in English, amusing herself with her store of peculiar Englishisms.

He mentioned the beheading—had she heard?

Yes, awful. And had he read that the Big Cheese in ISIS had said France was an evil and spiteful nation? 'Spiteful.' She repeated it. 'Such a strange word. La France as a spiteful woman. Lawrence said something similar.'

'D.H.?'

'No, darling, T.E. The *Seven Pillars* . . . one.'

She asked how his reading of the new Martin Amis was going.

He said he'd put it aside in favour of Lessing and Naipaul. 'But

I must go back to it. It feels like unfinished business.'

'Should I read it?'

'I'm not always sure what's going on. There are three first-person narrators.'

'*Merde!* Three's a crowd isn't it?'

After they'd rung off he sat with the phone in his hand, thinking that if they got divorced—properly divorced—they could have regular dinners together, as in the old days when they weren't fighting. They could tell one another about their work, and talk about books. He would like to tell her about Ray Parker's visit, and the 'truth' about his boyhood dream-girl who, according to Ray, was 'a Bitch with a very big B'.

And tell her that he would like to write poetry again (would he tell her about Helen White's excited discovery of his old poem?) but that he seemed for the moment to have lost the knack.

He imagined Louise sitting across the table in some nice neighbourhood restaurant, the Brasserie Balzar, for example, close to the Sorbonne, and asking him to explain what he meant by 'the knack'.

•

THE CONVERSATION WITH LOUISE HAD brought the Amis novel right back—urgently. The appetite to know how it would end had been aroused. The neurotic Auschwitz camp commandant Paul Doll, 'spearhead of this great national programme of applied hygiene' (as he described himself), had engaged the Jewish inmate Szmul to stab to death his unfaithful (both to him and to National Socialism) wife, Hannah. This was to happen on Walpurgisnacht. Szmul would be shot on the spot. His reward was that, the moment it was done, Doll would countermand an order against Szmul's wife, Shulamith. "'The only way you can save your wife," Doll said, "is by killing mine.'" As for Szmul's death, he was in Auschwitz and would die anyway. The death would be quick—quicker and less unpleasant than Zyklon B, which was the alternative.

So more than one outcome seemed possible, and Max read on now to find out 'what happens'. That, he decided—not Auschwitz, not the Holocaust, not the po-faced essay at the end of the book asking, How can we comprehend these century-defining events?— not these but the *story* was the guts of the matter. The big question was always the same: *What happens next? And how does it end?*

Was Amis aiming for the bigger prize? Forget the Booker. Why not the Nobel?

And in Stockholm for sure his name would come up from time to time. Some would say yes, some would say no—until . . .

Either 'young' Amis would die first, or he would get it. That was the story: the race against time. Would he win? Would it have an unlikely happy ending?

II.

SUMMER

LIGHTNING

4.

SLEEPING

AND WAKING

HELEN WHITE WAITED IN THE forecourt of the Gare de Lyon, keeping her eye on the clock in its tower with its beautiful, faintly blue face and ornate numbering. The train for Fontainebleau-Avon would go at two minutes past the hour. It was twenty minutes to. She was early. Max Jackson would be late—or he would not come at all. He'd said he would come but she was sure—almost sure— he would not. She repeated Zen lessons.

'Watch what you say, and whatever you say, do.

'Do not regret the past. Look to the future.

'Have the fearless face of a hero, and the loving heart of a child.'

She wondered whether she was confusing herself by mixing Gurdjieff with Zen; yet they seemed to go together, not to conflict.

She wondered what the Buddha had meant when he said he saw Nirvana as a nightmare of daytime.

It was ten to the hour, then five. No, Max would not come. She had bought two tickets . . .

She tried not to think, to achieve not-thinking, mindlessness, but her eyes were on the tower, the clock up there, waiting to hear it strike. Would she go without him?

And then he was there beside her, arriving from the other direction, the wrong, unexpected one. 'Quick,' she said. 'Downstairs . . .'

He was apologising for being late. And 'Tickets,' he said.

'I have them. Quickly, Max.'

They boarded the train just as the whistle was blown. They found a double seat and dumped themselves down, panting.

'I'm sorry,' he said again.

She had collapsed halfway over him, holding him by the shoulders. 'Don't be sorry.' And she pecked his cheek as she pulled herself into a sitting position. 'I knew you'd be dithering right up to the last minute.'

He didn't argue with that, and they sat, recovering, composing themselves. She pointed to the big yellow-striped bag at her feet. A baguette stuck out from its top and there were shapes, two bottles, fruit, other things . . . 'Picnic,' she said.

He nodded, smiling. 'Nice. I came in such a rush I brought nothing but a newspaper.'

'A newspaper,' she said. 'That's important.'

'In case we need to know what day it is?'

'And what's going on.'

Several kilometres clicked by. Feeling his warm thigh touching hers, she asked what Max was short for.

'Maxwell,' he said. And sang, '"Maxwelton's brae's are bonny where early fa's the dew."'

'Oh you sing in tune,' she said. 'And a nice—what are you—tenor? Baritone?'

'When my wife's feeling playful she calls me Maximus.'

'Maximus.'

'Playful or displeased. Sometimes both, of course.'

Helen nodded, approving. 'Max. Maxwell. Maximus. It's like conjugating a verb. Big Max, bigger Maxwell, and Maximus—biggest.' She gave this some thought. 'Funny word, big. Odd, I mean, when you say it over to yourself. Big. *Big*.'

'Bigger is odder,' Max said.

'And biggest . . . that's oddest.'

'Odd's pretty odd too,' Max said. 'Anglo-Saxon monosyllables. Like God . . . How odd of God . . .'

'Who chews the Jews.'

'To choose the Jews,' he corrected.

And they fell into another comfortable silence. What a strange young woman, he thought, and was pleased he'd come.

She told him about her recent discovery of Zen Buddhism. 'It's my new medication. I'm cutting down on the lithium. More Zen; less lithium.'

'Leth lithium,' he said. He asked was that safe and she said it was. She thought it was.

He said, 'But not instead of . . .'

'Not instead of. In addition to. Zen as supplement. Zen as additive.'

And more kilometres clicked by.

He held up his newspaper, which had a front-page shot of the French president in New York. 'I don't like him,' she said. 'I'm on Valérie's side.'

'Trierweiler? She's a very angry woman.'

'He lied to her.'

'About Julie Gayet. Of course he did.'

'Why "Of course"?'

'Because she's a very angry woman.'

'But he'd been unfaithful.'

Max shrugged. 'So he had something to hide.'

He told her that when he was young there was another socialist president of France—another François—Mitterrand. France was still testing nuclear bombs in the Pacific. Greenpeace had a ship, the *Rainbow Warrior*—had she heard about that?

'They were protesting about the bombs.'

'They were, and French secret agents blew it up—sank it in Auckland Harbour. I was a student at the time. I remember hearing the big boom, and then a few minutes later a second one, even bigger. It was late at night. I said to the girl I was in bed with that we were being attacked. I meant it as a joke, but it was true— sort of true. Most of the agents got away but two were caught.'

He told her the story—their conviction for manslaughter and how after that the Mitterrand government put economic pressure on New Zealand to release them.

'After a couple of years the government agreed they could serve out the rest of their sentence on an island in French Polynesia. As soon as they were there, France said they were unwell and had to be brought home.'

Their train ran on through the outskirts of Paris, past tall suburban houses and little tree-shaded villas, on, out into green countryside. Helen was quiet a while, and then asked, 'Was she nice?' He was unsure what she meant, and she said, 'When the bombs went off—the girl you were in bed with.'

'Oh . . . Yes, she was nice. She was very nice.'

'Where is she now?'

'Where indeed? Good question. Where do the dead go?'

Helen looked at him, frowning, trying to show the concern she felt for him, for his loss.

'Oh, it wasn't a tragedy,' he said. 'I mean it was, but not for me. We'd long since gone our separate ways. She married, had children—and then she died.'

The train rattled and clacked, rattled and clacked.

'Breast cancer,' he said. 'Thirty-nine.' Why was it important to get these things right? It wasn't, of course. And yes, he was sad about her death, but no need to say so.

Helen closed her eyes, listening. 'Did you know,' she said, 'that during the Battle of Waterloo a British soldier told the Duke of Wellington they had Napoleon in their gun-sights, and the Duke said it wasn't proper in war for commanders to be shooting at one another.'

Max laughed. 'No I didn't know that.' After a few seconds he said, 'Someone picked off Lord Nelson. He was a commander.'

'Different rules, do you think?'

She told him a story about a young Zen monk called Kitano who studied Chinese calligraphy and poetry, and grew exceptionally skilful at it, until his teacher praised him so highly Kitano thought, If I go on like this I'll be a poet, not a Zen teacher, so he gave up and never wrote another poem.

Max nodded, absorbing this. 'Is that a message for me?'

'I don't know. Is it?'

'I gave up poetry in favour of being a professor—is that it?'

'If the cap fits.'

'No I don't think it fits. The young monk—his was an act of will . . . A decision . . . A decision to stop writing poems.'

'Decisions are not always conscious, are they?'

His shrug might have been in disagreement, but he didn't argue.

At the Fontainebleau-Avon station a minibus was waiting to

gather those enrolled for the Gurdjieff tour. They drove no great distance to the building that had housed the institute, three storeys and quite grand, in beautiful grounds, now a block of apartments. Gurdjieff's home, a big wooden house, was next door. This whole complex was where the great man's devotees had come to live under his instruction, to learn 'wakefulness' rather than the 'sleep' which was, he argued, the norm for most human lives. They were to become 'conscious', to rid themselves of wasteful and negative emotions, to eschew regret, to shed 'personality', and to make their life's work the creation of a 'soul'. You were not born with a soul, but you could create one. That was the 'work'.

The tour commentary was partly a lesson. They had to imagine it all happening within these walls—the importance placed on very early rising, on chores and menial duties, on preparing meals, drawing water from the well, milking the cow, feeding the hens and finding their eggs, bee-keeping, and especially growing things; and then, in the evening, listening to a talk by the Master, which might be on any one of his favourite themes—the law of three, the law of seven, the four bodies of man, even 'Beelzebub'; and then would come the thrilling Sufi dancing, and the music.

They were shown the stairs where the writer Mansfield, one of the Master's better-known devotees, had had the tubercular haemorrhage that killed her. As the group moved on, Max hung back at the bottom of the oak-brown stairway with its heavy banister, and Helen waited at a discreet distance, thinking she was respecting an observance; but when he turned and hurried to catch up she saw he'd been checking his cell phone.

It was hot and they walked in the extensive gardens, rested under the trees, listened to further accounts of the institute's way of life; and then were set free to roam, to eat and drink whatever they'd brought for refreshment. Helen found a bower in the long grass under the shade of a tree, and opened the big bag with the yellow stripes, taking out two bottles of fruit juice, the baguette, which she broke into pieces, ham, cheese, tomatoes, two apples.

'A feast,' Max said. He lay in the grass, propped on one elbow.

'What are you thinking?' she said, hoping it might be about the Zen monk Kitano, so skilled when young, who stopped being a poet.

'Nothing. Not thinking.' He took a bite of the crusty bread. 'Just enjoying this good bread. Eat good bread, dear father. E.G.B.D.F. Did you ever learn the piano? I should have brought something.'

'You're here,' she said. 'That's your contribution. Imagine if I'd brought a picnic and you hadn't come . . .'

As she said it, she did imagine him *not* there—a space, an emptiness. It frightened her, because for a moment there *was* a space, just pressed-down grass and the trunk of a tree, where Max had been. She shivered. Perhaps he had no soul, it had not yet been created, and she had seen its absence. But then who had written that poem she so much admired? Where was the youthful Max's soul hiding? She would make it her project to find it, to bring it out.

When they had finished eating he sat up and brushed the crumbs away, then settled down again, his head resting on her thigh.

'Maximus,' she said, and laughed.

She had told him about her boyfriend in Oxford. 'This Hugh,' Max asked, 'is he a good guy? Does he treat you well?'

She said he was and he did, and she showed Max his photo on her cell phone.

'He looks OK,' Max said. 'In love with him, are you?'

She said it was hard to say. 'I suppose if it's anyone, it has to be Hugh.'

It sounded to Max as if she'd said, 'If it's anyone, it has to be you'—but he knew that was not what she would have said, or meant to say.

'But when you have my kind of head,' she went on, 'it's hard to put anything ahead of it.' And then, amused and distracted by the verbal echo, she said it again. 'Ahead of the head.'

'Makes you a bit of a solipsist,' Max said.

She laughed again and heard the laugh and noticed there was a bit of hysteria in it, because Max had that effect on her. 'Solipsist, yes. Soloist too,' she said. 'But I love my friends. I love the whole choir, really.'

His look was enquiring. What did that mean—the whole choir? But he didn't ask.

So they both dozed for a while in the warmth of summer and the scent of grass and flowers, but out of the sun, until the phone in his pocket buzzed him awake. He sat up, looking at it, stood up. 'I'll have to take this.'

As he walked to put a little distance between them she heard him say, '*Ça va?* How are things?' When he spoke next he was out of range. She could pick up only a word here and there, and the ups and downs, the recognisable roller-coaster of a conversation between a husband and a wife.

•

LOUISE WAS ASKING WHETHER HE could do a little research chore for her. 'There's a passage where Hélène Cixous compares Flaubert's style in *L'Éducation Sentimentale* with Clarice Lispector's in I'm not sure what. Possibly *A Breath of Life*. It's a male–female thing of course, and I can't find it in the books I have here.' She thought he might call in at the Sainte-Geneviève Library for her. 'I'd be so grateful, Max.'

He took a deep breath. He should not have taken the call. He said, 'There's always a queue.'

'Not at this time of year, darling. And I can't get away from here today.'

So he was darling when she wanted something. 'Tomorrow I could do it.'

'Tomorrow I could do it myself. I need it now.'

Only a wife would press like this—or a husband. Were they married or not? He'd thought not: not really; not any more. 'Sorry, Louise,' he said. 'I don't think I can . . .'

But the old habit persisted. 'Come on, Max. What's the problem? It's only a few blocks away.'

'Not from here it's not.'

'Where are you?'

Unable to think of a better answer, he said, 'Out of town.'

'Really? Out—how far?'

'Fontainebleau.'

'Why? What on earth are you doing?'

He thought of telling her that he and she now occupied separate apartments and separate beds precisely so that this kind of inquisition, of either party by the other, would not be necessary. But no, that would suggest he had something to hide, something to be ashamed of. He said, 'I'm learning about Gurdjieff. Did you know Katherine Mansfield couldn't decide whether he looked like a wise man or a carpet seller?'

'No, Max.' The voice was chilly. 'I didn't know that.'

'And then she died.'

'Yes?'

'Right here. It's a staircase.'

'A staircase. I see.' After a significant silence she said, 'So you can't hunt out that quotation for me.'

'I'll do my best, Louise. Depends on the trains. But if I can I will. I'll phone you tonight.'

Another silence. He knew he should end this conversation but he didn't want to. 'So . . .' he said.

'So are you going to tell me what you're doing?' And then, 'Who you're with?' And then once more, 'I know I have no right to ask.'

'I don't mind you asking. I only mind the conclusions you'll jump to. I'm with a student.'

Louise was on to it at once. 'The one who writes you letters?'

'One letter—yes, that one. And how do you know that?'

'You left it on your table.'

'And you read it.'

'No. Certainly not. You know I wouldn't do that. It was open. I saw her name at the bottom of the page—Helen someone.'

'Of Troy. Yes, that's her.'

'You're a fool, Max.'

'She's English. She's had a few problems. She needs help—a sympathetic ear, that's all.'

'At Fontainebleau?'

'It's the summer *vac*, isn't it? We had a picnic.'

'What kind of problems?'

'Mental . . .'

'Max . . .'

'I don't mean she's mad . . .' As he said this he remembered she'd said that's exactly what she was: mad.

'And you're with this disturbed young woman—'

'She's not disturbed.'

'Learning about that fraudulent Russian . . .'

'Gurdjieff. Was he Russian?'

'Armenian mother. Greek father.'

Oh for God's sake, how did she know *that*? He wouldn't ask.

'I'm sure it sounds odd, Louise . . .'

But there was a click and she was gone.

●

THEY WERE TAKEN NEXT TO the Gurdjieff grave in the local cemetery. It was a large, level raised oblong in grass, with a border of flowers and a massive rough-cut stone at either end. There was a small stone seat where you could think about the man in the ground under you, and his philosophy and what he meant when he said 'I cannot die'.

The guide explained that you could spread a cloth on the grave and it would absorb something of the *Kaife* that would come up through the ground from his body—the emanation of his great spirit.

Helen told Max that devotees would sometimes bring cloths ornately woven in bright colours for this purpose; and one or two of their group did have rather superior-looking pieces of coloured silk which they laid out reverently. Helen had only a fine, beautifully laundered and ironed cotton handkerchief, yellow and gold, which she spread on the grass.

'They could have buried a horse in there,' Max said looking at the size of the grave. 'Even lying on its side.'

While she listened to the guide, he wandered about among the graves. Only a few metres away from Gurdjieff he found Katherine Mansfield. The inscription said 'Katherine Mansfield, Wife of John Middleton Murry'. It didn't mention that she was a writer.

There were a few delays on the line and the journey back to the Gare de Lyon took more than an hour, by which time it was too late for a visit to the Sainte-Geneviève. Max's sunburnt face was hot. His head throbbed faintly. He felt he'd been foolish, and yet he argued with himself. Why foolish? As he'd said to Louise, it was summer, wasn't it? The sun was shining, the flowers were out, the countryside was lovely. What harm had been done?—unless it was harm to his wife's French bourgeois sense of propriety; to the necessary grandeur of the professorial role. Yes, that was it, undoubtedly.

Louise had unsettled him; but when Helen told him she lived in the rue Parrot, just a short walk from the station, and suggested he should come in and have a cup of tea—or even a bowl of pasta, if he felt like staying a while—he said, very properly, even primly, that tea would be nice.

The apartment, five floors up in a rickety lift, was very small, long and narrow like a railway carriage, with two windows on one side, a divan-bed on the other against the wall, a small table and two chairs at the far end, an alcove kitchen at the other, and cubicle *douche et WC* as in a one- or two-star Paris hotel. 'Dinky', she called it, and it was, especially with her decorations, which he was invited to admire—a modest couple of bookshelves, seashells, a single Roman tile, a Japanese glass paperweight, a framed photo of a mill-house and millstream with trailing willows, and one of what appeared to be an English country rail-stop with the sign ADLESTROP.

There was no space for easy chairs, and hardly room to pass one another between the windows and the divan, which though placed longwise was quite broad. In fact, with its bright orange cotton cover, the divan (where obviously she slept—there was nowhere else that would serve) dominated the room and made everything else subsidiary. The windows, pushed open, looked out on the black slate roof, ending in the rainwater guttering, and beyond that, five storeys down, was the rue Parrot.

She pushed him into a sitting position on the divan, took three steps into the kitchen to fill the kettle and switch it on, and three steps back to dump herself down beside him. She's very vigorous, he thought.

'Don't be alarmed,' she said, as if he'd spoken the thought aloud and she was answering.

He had not been alarmed but thought perhaps he ought to be.

'Come on,' she said. 'Relax. You're all tense. Look at you.' And then, laughing, 'Relax, Max. *Relax!*'

Her fingers were on his throat, his face, his head. 'Close your eyes. That's right.' She ran fingers delicately over his eyes and up into his hair; then down over his ears to neck and shoulders.

'Lie face down,' she said. 'Let me give you a massage.'

He allowed himself to be pushed forward on to his front. She lifted his lower legs up on to the divan and pulled his shirt up from under his belt. Then, kneeling on the floor beside him, she began to massage his back.

The kettle whistled and she paused to turn it off.

Now she climbed on to the divan with him, knelt beside him, then straddled him with her knees, and applied strong hands, strong fingers, to his back, to every inch of it, to his neck and up into his scalp.

'I like this,' he said, surrendering to sensation.

'Of course you do. Everybody does.'

Helen's hands moved up to the back of his neck again. 'You're relaxing,' she said. 'I can feel it.'

He drifted, and for a brief time slept, then woke feeling her no longer massaging, but lying right over him, her limbs loose. Perhaps she too was asleep. Yes she was—she was sleeping—he could tell by the even, just-audible sound of her breathing, with a small whistle at the end of each breath. He could feel her breasts against his back and wondered why he hadn't noticed them. They felt quite large.

They must be the broadly rounded kind, not pointy.

He was thinking in a rather uncertain way of the Gurdjieff doctrine that ordinary lives were a 'sleep' and that 'wakefulness' had to be worked for, worked *at*. And then of Shakespeare's 'sleep that knits up the ravelled sleeve of care', which merged into what were really just words—misty, mysterious, meaningless . . .

Then he really did sleep.

•

THAT NIGHT—BUT IN FACT IT was early morning—Max walked all the way back to the 5th arrondissement. As he marched along he sang aloud, as people sometimes did in the street outside his apartment, French songs, English songs. There was one about Paris in the early morning, '*Il est cinq heures, Paris s'éveille*'; but the one he kept coming back to was Joe Dassin's '*Aux Champs-Élysées*', another of the discs Helen had played on her little machine. He could remember some lines, not others, but always the refrain.

A light rain was falling. He stopped and sat on a bollard and rolled up his right trouser leg a few turns to look at his new ankle tattoo, which was beginning to hurt again. But it was swathed in gladwrap and he couldn't admire the image. They had said it wouldn't bleed, and so far there didn't seem to be any blood. He was surprised to have done this, but not sorry. With Helen's encouragement he had chosen an image of an owl, a small owl with round, staring eyes. The tattooist had drawn it on first with biro, and then gone to work with the electric tool. He had warned Max that it would hurt, and it had, but not too much.

The owl: wisdom. Who was it said or wrote, 'It is only at the hour of darkness that the owl of Minerva descends'? Was it Hegel? Yes, he thought so. Hegel would do.

Which, he wondered now, had been his own hour of darkness? The rift with Louise? The banishment downstairs? Where, in that case, was the wisdom? How would it arrive? Helen had been sure it would come in the form of a poem—a new one.

He pressed on with his walk. He was happy. Helen, the 'mad' young Englishwoman, the self-described Romantic, had made him happy. She had reminded him of Wordsworth's lines about Chatterton, 'the marvellous boy' who had written brilliant poems and presented them as rediscovered masterpieces of an earlier time, and then killed himself.

> We poets in our youth begin in gladness
> But thereof come in the end despondency and madness.

It ought to have been a gloomy reminder, a clumsily written warning, but she had delivered it, and he had received it, in a spirit of celebration. They had drunk a lot by then, and eaten well, and he had been indiscreet—had told her about being in love with Sylvie Renard, and about the difficulties of marriage to a distinguished French professor from a family who were 'names'.

Did it matter? No it didn't matter; or not much.

Summer was making strategic advances through the streets and gardens, and in a few hours Paris would be bright and loud again, busy and pleased to be Paris—'Nobody's dream but your own', as he had written in that long-ago poem—but everyone's dream too.

•

A DAY OR SO LATER and morning 'at good hour', as the French say, Max was in his office intending to gather and reorder his Lessing-Naipaul file. The work was getting nearer to what he wanted it to be—something that would be quite modest in size, precise, tightly written, fresh and intelligent. But Julien Lemont was here already; Max had not expected that, especially not so early.

Julien was on his feet and stamping about. He was working on the department's timetable for the new term—ahead of time, but that was how it had to be. Problems had to be foreseen and ironed out. Everyone, wherever they were, at home or on holiday, could be reached online or by cell phone. Everyone had expressed a preference and these, put together into the computer, amounted to an impossibility—a series of impossibilities—a mess.

'No one,' Julien said, 'should have been invited to state a preference. Half of them are living in Paris, with a holiday cottage or a *gîte* somewhere in the wilds they want to get away to for weekends. The other half are living in the wilds and only want to be in Paris three days a week. Everybody wants to teach Tuesday, Wednesday, Thursday.'

Max said, 'Tell them sorry, you've tried and it can't be done. Here's the schedule. And then send any howls of protest upstairs.'

'That's what it will come down to.'

He sat down, sighed heavily. 'Fuck,' he said wearily, and reached out a hand to Max. 'How are you, friend?'

'I'm good,' Max said. 'I'm well. I suspect I'm even exceptionally well.'

'Yes I can see that. I can hear it in your voice. What happened? You get laid?'

'Like an egg, yah? No. Not quite. Not really. Had a massage.'

'Happy ending?'

'I just got lucky, Jay.'

'You want to tell me the story?'

'Not now. Got some work to do here.'

'Go to it, man. I'll be wordless.'

And they did—worked at their separate tasks until 10.30, when they stopped for coffee. Julien sat up straight, stretching his back. 'Some of this will come out as people want,' he said. 'The rest will have to suck the lemon.'

He had a packet of chocolate biscuits in his desk to have with the coffee which they brewed there in the office. 'Tell me about Lessing,' he said.

'Lessing's not a puzzle,' Max said. 'Easy to see why she got the Nobel. In fact, it's surprising it took so long. It's poor old Naipaul I'm struggling with. I've just fought my way through *The Enigma of Arrival.* The publishers put it out as a novel, but it's really autobiography—and not *interesting*, you know, in the way autobiography should be. Nothing happens to the guy. He just sweats it out being a writer, doesn't mention his wife—and goes for *walks*! It's all about next to nothing except the pain of it all—and set in rural England. Listen to this.'

He picked up the green-covered book from his desk and read, '"The noblest impulse of all—the wish to be a writer, the wish that had ruled my life—was the most imprisoning, the most insidious, and in some ways the most corrupting."'

'That's dark,' Julien said.

A moment later they were talking about French politics. *Le Figaro* was quoting Jacques Chirac as supporting Alain Juppé to be the centre-right candidate for the 2017 elections. His wife, Bernadette, disagreed. She'd told *Le Canard Enchaîné* that Juppé was 'a very cold fish' and she would prefer Nicolas Sarkozy. Their daughter Claude was denying that she'd been Sarkozy's mistress for a brief time after her husband died. She agreed with her father and supported Juppé.

'What's happened to French politics?' Max said. 'It used to be so buttoned up.'

'France is taking her clothes off,' Julien said.

'And now there's Depardieu's—what would you call it? Autobiography? Confession?'

'Fourteen bottles of wine in one day. I'd call that a lie.'

•

SYLVIE ARRIVED EARLY AT THE Opéra Bastille. She bought a programme and picked up the tickets that had been booked weeks ago online. Bertholdt would be ten minutes behind her. She thought of a drink in the bar, but didn't want to have it alone. She found an empty seat in the foyer and began to read the programme notes.

She became conscious of someone standing in front of her. She tried to read on. The figure did not move. She sensed his urgency, and yet reluctance, or inability, to speak. She glanced up. It was Max Jackson. He was red-faced, bushy-haired and untidy.

'Max!' She stood up and they embraced without touching. 'What are you doing here?'

'Well, I . . .'

He was dressed informally, not for the opera. He seemed flustered. She laughed. 'They're after you, aren't they?'

'Who?'

'The Eumenides? The Mafia?' And then, risking it, 'Your wife?'

But whatever it was that was troubling him, he couldn't rise to jokes. 'I was passing . . .'

Passing? What was he talking about? To be here in the foyer he must have climbed all those stairs or come up from street level in a lift.

'Where's Bertholdt?' he said.

'Bertholdt's on his way. He'll be here in a few minutes.' She thought a moment and asked, 'Why were you passing?' She tried not to give the word an ironic or totally disbelieving ring.

'You told me Bertholdt was taking you to *Tosca*.'

So he had come in pursuit? This was exciting.

'Everyone seems to be going off for the summer break . . . So there's not a lot of time.'

'For what, Max?'

'We made our decisions about the World War One conference. I'm worried it hasn't gone forward.'

'The call for papers has gone out.' She thought he knew this.

He said, 'I could have sent you an email but I thought it was important to see you—just to stress . . .'

'Urgency?'

'Yes. Well—not exactly. And it's good you feel it's all in hand. It shouldn't be allowed just to slide until we're back in harness.'

He seemed to have recovered some of his authority. That was better. She preferred him like that.

She said, 'There's definite interest—from both sides of the Channel. I'll do you a little report and email it to everyone.'

'Good,' he said. 'Excellent.' And then, looking down, 'So those are the shoes. Good choice!'

She laughed. 'How clever of you to remember. And to notice. I bought this *foulard* too.'

'Oh that's beautiful. Another good choice.'

They were smiling at one another. He said, 'There's something else.'

'Yes,' she said. 'I think there is.'

'You and I—we need to meet and talk. Not about war poets. About us.'

'Good,' she said. 'Let's do it.' She squeezed his hand. 'You've got my email.'

'I'll suggest a time. You were going to play the piano for me.'

'I was and I will. I'll suggest a place.'

They were still smiling when Bertholdt arrived. He looked from one to the other. 'Am I interrupting?'

'Must rush,' Max said. He grabbed Bertholdt's hand and shook it. 'Nice to see you, Herr Volker. Au revoir, Sylvie,' kissing her on one side only. Well meant but not well aimed, it brushed her ear rather than her cheek. Then he was gone, leaving her alone with Bertholdt, who was looking at her now with a faintly ironic smile as if he didn't need to say it: I know you so well.

'Max is in a pickle,' she said.

'I could see. What's his problem?'

'Oh nothing really important. Panic about the conference—planned, and then not enough done.'

'Why not an email?'

'Exactly. But you know how it is. Too many emails flying around and they get overlooked, forgotten.'

Bertholdt nodded, looked at his watch, and then, casually, 'Is he in love with you?'

'Jesus, Bertholdt! I hope not.'

'What about you?'

'What?'

'Are you in love with him?'

'Don't be silly,' she said, and then, 'No.'

'He's a weird guy.'

'You think? Yes, maybe.'

'You said you liked him.'

'I do. He's nice. He's bright.' She smiled. 'And he's my senior. Bosses can be bastards. He's a good one.'

'Did I tell you I met him eating in the Boul' Mich at that place called Il Palazzo? Right out in the street. Reading a novel about

Auschwitz.'

'Really? Oh but that's the new—'

'Martin Amis. Yes but he had to tell me about it.'

'What do you mean?'

'That I'm German. Guilty party. The usual.'

'Oh no, Bertholdt.'

'Oh yes, Sylvie.'

'I'm sure not.'

'Believe me . . .'

'I believe you thought so. But come on, B. Do you think he stationed himself out there, reading a book about the Holocaust, just so he could catch you going by?'

'No of course not, but it's called never missing an opportunity.'

'And that's called paranoia.'

'Very British.'

'Very German.'

And then, taking his arm, she said, 'Come on, darling. Don't let Max Jackson spoil our evening. Aren't you waiting for the stars to be brightly shining?'

'Just before I'm shot—yes, for sure. Did you pick up the tickets?'

She produced them from her purse and he took them in that cool, commanding way she liked to joke was his SS manner, but which she sometimes thought might be what she liked most about him.

5.

SUMMER

LIGHTNING

FOR MAX, UNCLE HENRI'S FUNERAL was a particular kind of ordeal—a familiar, familial kind, but one he'd had a rest from since the move downstairs. It had partly to do with being the father of French children who, when he arrived upstairs to get into his 'funeral' suit, were quarrelling fiercely about whose turn it was to clean the fish tank in the roof garden—in schoolyard French so rapid and totally idiomatic he caught the drift often without the detail.

There was anger on both sides and he told them they should try to be nice to one another.

The quarrel stopped and he saw them both staring at him. It was a look he often noticed, even though he spoke to them mostly in French. Maybe all children looked at their parents like that at certain moments: the bigs, the bosses, the aliens. But he thought there was something extra in his case that put him at a further distance. It was the French language, which he could say he spoke, he understood, he used—but he had learned it first in the wrong way, off the page, not through the ear, and at an age when whatever you learn tends to stick: you don't easily unlearn it. For him English was like wind in the trees, a running river or, simply, music. It was something *heard*. He'd learned it as you learn a melody—by ear, and 'by heart'. French was something *seen*. For Max it could never be entirely parted from its signs and symbols. Language began in the ears. The blind from birth, he sometimes reminded Louise when they argued about this, learn to talk like everyone else; the deaf from birth do not.

That moment had given him today's first real look at the children. They were extraordinary—one hazel-eyed, the other brown, and both beautiful. Louise had dressed them to be seen, to be admired, by the family of course but by 'all the world', as one says in French. Julie's dress was frilly, in a pale, super-subtle yellow which seemed to faint on the threshold of green, and with a matching rosebud in her hair. Jean-Claude was in his very best young chap's bracks and jacket, but wearing a straw hat with a broad curling brim and a leather thong under the chin. Max could see the boy was unhappy with it, as he would have been himself at that age.

They took a taxi to the church, Saint-Étienne-du-Mont. It was no great distance and they could have walked, but Louise didn't relish the thought of climbing that hill; and in any case she felt it would be quite wrong for the family to see them arriving on foot. There was also the wind: she didn't want her coiffure *dérangée*. (Deranged hair—it had been one of their inter-language jokes, like Floe-Bert.)

As the taxi pulled up in front of the church Louise noticed that

Jean-Claude had removed the hat. It was now hanging by its thong down his back. She told him to put it back on his head—and with the glum compliance of the French child which Max always found surprising, he did.

Funeral cars were angle-parked ready for the drive to Montparnasse. On a paved area below the steps to the church doors were family and friends, greetings and surprise (or pretended surprise) encounters, with embraces where neither one touched the other, but the side-to-side movements from the waist were sweeping, and as coolly expressive as the rituals of mating swans. Max stood back watching it, like the performance of a play. In the background, hardly more than a hundred metres away, the Panthéon was swathed in images of many faces, a veritable crowd, while underneath the wrapping something restorative was being done to its tower.

Indoors those most closely connected to the deceased, the truly bereaved, including the resented second wife and the resentful daughters by the first, were already in their places at the front. Their ages, the widow and the daughters, were about the same. Louise and her family were led in and down the aisle by an attendant in undertaker's attire; but she thanked him and veered off to the right, avoiding (Max supposed) close contact with those who disapproved of her and might not welcome her claiming a place among them.

Max had been in this church before, but had forgotten how extraordinary it was, with its curves of carved stone on either side swirling like lace curtains up to a lateral bridge of the same stone, this in turn supporting the crucifix elevated high against the principal stained-glass window of the apse. He remembered the bust of Racine, and near it, one of Pascal; and that out in the enclosed churchyard at the back was the grave of Jean-Paul Marat, revolutionary supporter of the *sans-culottes* whom Charlotte Corday stabbed in his bath.

They settled into their places, enfolded in the spooky whispers and hushed assurances of the organ. To their right was a chapel in which marble figures enacted the entombment of Jesus—four women, Mary distraught at the centre, comforted by one of the disciples, two men lowering the body into the tomb.

Now the officiating priest spoke in welcome and reminder that their purpose was to celebrate, and thank God for, the gift the life of Henri had been. Max was unsure how each of the priests he could see ranked, but there were a number of them, and he assumed their colourful presence, the incense, the massive bouquets of flowers, the hefty, ornate coffin, the obsequious and lugubrious funeral directors, not to mention the cars to Montparnasse and the opening of the family vault there, would all have cost the family. He wondered whether Louise had contributed, assumed she had, and resolved he would not ask.

He glanced along the row at Jean-Claude and Julie. They sat very properly, still and even attentive. They had been baptised Catholic. Louise had insisted on that. They had even had a first communion, dressed in white, and with infant hands pressed together in prayer. All of this had been on the understanding that Max, as their father, would not pretend to faith of any kind—any more than Louise herself would acknowledge more than loyalty to family and social convention.

But the children, he supposed, were familiar with the language they were hearing now, about God giving his only begotten Son ('begotten'?—Max gave that a passing moment's thought), the Son's hideous execution and the consequent forgiveness of sins and 'life everlasting', where they could expect the joyful surprise of seeing Uncle Henri again. All that was required was belief. You had to believe—that was the small price for entry into the uncommon market of the Divine Kingdom. Strange how Jesus had insisted upon this and on nothing else. It was every Messiah's requirement: believe in me—not 'please', but 'or else'.

Max had an anxious thought that this might be like learning French first by ear rather than off the page—too early for the effect ever to be quite expunged. He resolved to talk to the children about it one day soon to ensure that none of it was becoming what was called 'deep faith'. He had made resolutions like this before and had not acted on them. He promised himself he would do better; would be a better guide and protector.

Now came the Mass, and he watched as his family went up to kneel with the faithful at the altar rail and receive the wafer on the tongue and the sip of wine. While this went on an amplified female voice was singing, 'Here is the body and the blood of the Lord, the cup of salvation and the bread of life. Eternal God gives himself as food so we may have eternal life.' '*Nourriture*'—food. Max's shudder was one of distaste.

Once outside, Louise approached the bereaved—the widow, the daughters, a surviving aunt—with an hauteur that matched their own. It was a competition, but one in which each side acknowledged the other's status. Uncle Henri's family would not have forgotten 'the picture'. Indeed it would be at the forefront of their minds—Louise's too. All that was in the air around them as they and Louise embraced and exchanged their murmured condolences. Max was in a special category, neither 'inside' nor 'outside' all this, and treated, therefore, with politesse rather than hauteur.

He thought about these words. They were subtly different from their English equivalents. Politeness meant the same and yet not quite: there was something casual about politeness when compared with *politesse* which, with its terminal susurrus, had a certain extra . . . What could you call it but finesse? And for *hauteur* there was no English equivalent. Haughtiness was too close, aurally, to naughtiness to be taken seriously. Disdain was too strong. *Hauteur* was *le mot juste*. Where would English be without its supplements, its toppings or top-ups, of French? And why did the French resist the mix, as if it were a kind of contagion? *Vive la différence!* And among the European languages it was English, the mongrel, that flourished.

One of a fleet of funeral cars took them on from church to cemetery. It was no great distance, through a warren of small streets and out into the Boulevard Saint-Michel, then down to Montparnasse and through the cemetery's massive gates into a cobbled way lined with family tombs which the French called *chapelles*.

Max found himself on the outer edge of the small crowd. From where he stood it appeared that Uncle Henri was to be left on an upper shelf in the mausoleum. Whether that would be final, or functionaries would return later to sort out that macabre interior before the final locking of its iron door, was not clear. But the terminal blessing was being said over him by a priest in a small black skull cap; so perhaps that was indeed the end for Uncle, and he was to spend eternity on a high shelf.

Later, at home, Max tried to tell Louise about his anxieties during the service.

But it had just been a funeral, she said. Something had to be done when someone died. 'Just think of it as an observance.'

'Based on untruths.'

She shrugged. The French shrug that had once seemed charming; he'd grown to dislike it. 'So we can all look forward to being greeted by Uncle in eternity.'

'A figure of speech,' she said.

'An untruth.'

'Don't be such a puritan, Max. No harm's done.'

'Science when it matters, and religion when it doesn't . . .'

'Have faith at least in your children's intelligence. They're bright kids. They'll sort these things out.'

'And it's all in such execrable taste.'

She laughed. It was a frosty laugh. 'I'm always amused when you reveal that you're a snob.'

She used the English word and he asked what on earth she meant.

'The snobbery of good taste,' she said.

'Oh that? Yes, I hope so.'

She turned away with an impatient gesture. It was a marker he recognised from many arguments. He thought of it as the end of Louise's tether. He was angry for a moment, then sorry for her.

He put a hand on her arm. 'You should have married a Frog.'

'There's no guarantee of a good outcome with Frogs,' she said, 'except in the fairy tales where they turn into princes.' She patted the hand. 'I suppose there might have been fewer misunderstandings. Should you have married an Englishwoman?'

He remembered his thoughts about language, but that was difficult territory. 'A New Zealander perhaps,' he said, and they smiled at one another as if it had been a joke.

•

DOWNSTAIRS MAX WENT TO THE window and looked out on the little courtyard where he kept a small garden with a few reminders of home—a flax bush, whose Latin name, absurdly remembered from primary-school days (another example of the power of early learning) was *Phormium tenax*; a kōwhai which produced a few yellow bells in spring but did not flourish; a mānuka whose tiny leaves he crushed for their scent, to remind himself of childhood; and a lemon-scented verbena, also for its scent of his childhood, though its origins he thought might be European. The courtyard was dominated by three medium-sized trees, one he recognised as a plane, the others he had never enquired about—just trees, he would have said, very nice ones, doing all the things European trees do, having been designed to vary appropriately with the seasons, which the evergreens of the southern hemisphere declined to do. Clearly God lived north of the equator. Conifers were an exception, and provided trees for Christmas.

A light shower was falling, the kind that made his herbaceous and aromatic mementoes appear melancholy. Maybe he should plant something assertively French there. What might that be? The area was mostly paved and there was only a small garden space, but it was surprising how if you pushed plants hard up against one another they would compete for the light and wouldn't easily give up.

The woman across the courtyard was looking out too, and they waved to one another and smiled. She pointed up to the sky and gave a resigned shrug. He nodded and pulled a face that said something like, 'Yes, it's disappointing.'

Politesse, he thought. And then, neighbourliness: was there a French equivalent? *Esprit de voisinage*, but that was rather cold and formal.

He took an umbrella and hoped to sneak out unseen, but Skipper saw him and clamoured to come too, even racing to get his leash and bring it. So the leash was hooked on to his harness and they went together, out through the big gate and along the street to the bar-tabac of Georges Constant, whose wife was Louise's *femme de ménage*. She was at the counter, Gina from Italy, with her French husband, Georges, who liked to tell his nicotine-addicted customers that such a cloud had fallen over the trade in cigarettes and tobacco he was thinking of 'taking his pile' and retiring with Gina to Senigallia, her home town on the Adriatic coast. It was a kind of threat he hung over them, as if access to their drug would vanish with him if they didn't remain faithful, and even buy more. He had thought of taking out a licence to sell the electronic smokes that were becoming fashionable, but decided against it: one half of the business would have been in competition with the other, in the end to the detriment of both.

He brought this idea of retirement up now with Max, who was not a smoker, however. 'I could become a fisherman,' he said. 'It's all E.C. now isn't it? One community.'

'One community and not enough fish,' Max said. 'You might starve.'

Georges nodded and pulled a long face. 'No smoking and not enough fish—what a world!'

'You're looking very smart, Monsieur,' Gina said.

Max looked down at his suit. 'A funeral,' he said. 'Louise's uncle Henri.'

'Oh sad,' she said, taking her tone from him, recognising that there was no need for heavy condolences with this one. 'Nice suit, though. Good to have an excuse to wear your best.'

'Gets it out of the moth bag,' Max agreed.

He told her how long the family were to be away and that she needed only to clean the big apartment once. Skipper would go with them. Max himself would be mostly at home; but she would need to feed the pigeons on the roof garden, and the fish in the pond up there. And keep an eye on the pot plants in case they needed watering.

'Make sure the netting stays in place over the fish pond. And don't over-feed the fish.'

Yes, she knew all that and wouldn't forget. She had noted their return date and would see there were basic supplies in the fridge up there. 'And for you, Monsieur—no vacation?'

'I'm writing a book. I'd like to finish it.'

Gina looked as if this troubled her. It was not the normal order. Usually the family went on their summer holiday together. She preferred things to be as they had been, not as they might be. It occurred to Max that she would not want to return to Senigallia.

'We're in for rain here,' Georges said, 'but down there on the coast the sun will be shining.'

'Au revoir, Skeep-aire,' Gina called after them.

'Gina the cleaner,' Max said to himself. He wondered how much she knew about his and Louise's estrangement. Louise was not a confider, but it was surprising what a middle-class Frenchwoman would tell her *femme de ménage*.

•

LOUISE HAD FINISHED HER EDITING and the text was ready to go to the publisher. Her introduction, which she had asked Max to read and comment on, had taken issue in particular with Roland Barthes' complaint about what he called the 'Flaubertisation' of literature. Barthes had argued that Flaubert, writing letters telling his friends how he had spent a whole night searching for a single adjective, a day writing a sentence, a week on a paragraph or a page, had elevated the idea of 'style', and the quest for '*le mot juste*', into a holy grail, encouraging the belief that hard work and protracted application were the sole means to the end of Art. Gone was the notion of the Muse, 'inspiration', the inexplicable *donnée*, the gift of genius. These were deceptions, romantic delusions. Writers, according to Flaubert (or according to Flaubert according to Barthes), were solo practitioners, sentenced to home detention and hard labour, and the figure most likely to come to the door to spur them on was not the Muse but the debt collector. This was their distinction and their glory.

Louise disagreed.

She said Flaubert had never claimed, or thought, that he was laying down laws for fine writing. He had only been describing how it came about for him. It was possible, she conceded, writers being competitive, that he'd had one eye on Balzac's ease and speed of composition, partly envious, partly disapproving, and not unwilling to benefit from the comparison if it should be made in his favour. But if writers who came after Flaubert had made a fetish of the idea of style, and had even elevated it into the principle of Art for Art's Sake, that was not something for which he could be blamed.

And the end for Flaubert had been an achieved clarity, intelligibility, elegance. Against this, Roland Barthes had favoured the obscurity of the New Wave novels of Claude Simon and Alain Robbe-Grillet, which he preferred because he saw clarity as the writer imposing himself or herself upon you, giving you no room to move. In the obscure and the oblique lay finally the 'death of the author' and the emancipation of the reader. By uncertainty about what the thing you were reading meant, you were freed to make new meanings, new interpretations, and so to become yourself the author of the work.

Against Barthes and his kind, Louise spoke up for precision, for style, for Flaubert. In the current literary climate, which seemed to be tending against the opacity of the New Wave novels of the 1960s and '70s, Flaubert's flag could be flown again with renewed confidence rather than at half-mast. Louise's edition would help to restore his reputation.

Max, she knew, felt no great enthusiasm for Floe-Bert. That might be his anglophone prejudice; or just a matter of individual temperament. But she also knew he was sincere when he told her that her introduction was good. 'In fact it's better than good,' he told her. 'I'm full of admiration—and envy, Louise. It's brilliant.'

She gave him a hug, and her eyes (face turned away so he wouldn't see) filled with tears. She had needed that. Now she could send it on its way.

•

MAX WAS ALREADY OUT OF bed when the midnight storm broke. He was in pyjamas, making himself a pot of tea and a slice of toast. He'd found, since moving out of the upstairs apartment, his night habits had changed. Whereas once, waking, he would have lain there trying to sleep again, not wanting to disturb Louise, now he moved about freely, turning on lights and going from room to room. If he felt like reading, he read; if he felt like eating and drinking tea, he would do that. It was freedom; it was also disorder, and he sometimes felt nostalgia for the old regime.

Waiting for the kettle to boil, he pulled up the right pyjama leg, exposing his ankle tattoo. The owl of Minerva. It looked very good, very neat; but he was glad not to have to explain to Louise how it had come about.

He was in a comfortable chair with the curtains open and interior lights out, taking his tea, enjoying fresh buttered toast, when the first big flash broke the night, lighting up the garden, followed by the thunder crack. It made his mind leap back almost thirty years to his time as a student and the house he'd grown up in. It was a villa, with a lawn, flower beds and scented shrubs at the front and vegetables at the back, and a security light which came on when anyone came through the gate at night. It was late, as now, and the security light was coming on, staying on its due minute, and switching itself off again—and then, almost at once, on again. Max had gone to his bedroom window at the front of the house to look out. The light, turned on by any movement in the garden, was being triggered by a hedgehog moving about. He had encountered this little nocturnal animal before—in fact had named it after a teacher with bristly red hair who had been known to the boys at his school as Hedgie Boulton. So the hedgehog, invisible by day, roaming the garden at night in search of slugs and snails and whatever else hedgehogs ate, was named Boulton, and was causing the light to come on, not once but repeatedly. In fact, Max decided, Boulton had learned the trick of turning it on, which he did by surprisingly quick little sprints—not because he needed the light to see his prey, but just for the hell of it, as some birds seem to enjoy gliding for the pleasure of gliding, and dolphins and porpoises appear to leap out of the sea for the pleasure of leaping. Boulton was turning the light on because he could and it was fun.

Boulton must have been a lady—Mrs Boulton—because Max had once seen her carrying her baby in her mouth, a small, prickly brown bundle, transferring it from one part of the garden to another.

Max sat in his armchair now, watching lightning flash-flood the courtyard, remembering his student years, and wishing it could have been a hedgehog causing his small New Zealand plantation to light up here in Paris. Somewhere in wider France he supposed there must be hedgehogs, but not here. Perhaps in the Luxembourg Gardens? Or (more likely) the Jardin des Plantes?

The rain got heavier, the flashes brighter, the thunder louder, and he settled into it, into the feeling that, though separated by a double pane of glass, he was somehow *in* it, *in* the natural world, not in Paris. Out in the wilds somewhere with wild Sylvie. Was she wild? Would she be?

And then his mind switched abruptly to Louise's essay, and what she had written about Roland Barthes. And then to Barthes himself, mother-obsessed in his private life, the super Post-Modernist critic, hell-bent on cleaning up the French—indeed the world—literary scene, who had died (supreme irony) after being run down by a laundry van.

•

HELEN WHITE WAS FRIGHTENED OF many things, and especially of thunder and lightning. But to be afraid was not altogether a bad thing. Sometimes it could be enjoyed, like a new taste, a piquant flavour, a subtle aroma, a bad smell.

She was standing at her windows on the sixth floor looking out over the rue Parrot and the roofs of Paris, remembering the joke she'd thought of with Max Jackson and had suppressed, though she hadn't been able to suppress the laugh that came with it—that he was married to *Flaubert's Parrot*. It was the name of a novel by Julian Barnes, and of course Max would know that, so he would have 'got' the joke, but she hadn't quite had the courage to make it.

She tried to enter into her favourite fantasy of herself, that she was a male writer, an older man, old, Willie Yeats perhaps.

> I the poet Willie Yeats
> With old mill boards and sea-green slates
> And smithy work from the Gort Forge
> Restored this tower for my wife, George.

Funny to have a wife called George, she thought.

> And may these characters remain
> When all is ruin once again.

Or maybe Ezra Pound in his very old age, lined and grizzled as he had been in those shots of him in Venice with his American girlfriend Olga Rudge. Old Olga! A violinist, and brave. She'd given a public recital at Rapallo, and then put on her walking shoes and hitched up her skirts for the climb up the walking track through olive groves to her house in the hills—the one Ezra had celebrated in *The Cantos* as 'Circe's Ingle'.

Old Ezra had been exceptionally silly—the anti-Semite, the know-all, the braggart, the bossy-boots. She remembered reading somewhere that he'd thought of Mussolini as 'an Artist' because he played the violin. That would have been Olga's influence.

To be old and unwise and a writer it might be necessary to be silly—even very silly. Helen could accept that. It was her alternative self. It gave her pleasure and took away her fears of thunder and lightning, which might otherwise have been the voice of the gods up there, angry and threatening. Worse: the voice of old man One-God, the One you couldn't trust, the Big Old Boy, World-Flooder, Smiter of Everyone, even the Jews, who were supposed to be the ones he chose: His chosen People. How odd of God . . .

She thought of T.S. Eliot and the batty woman in *The Waste Land* who says she's going to rush out into the street with her hair down; the one who asks him what he's thinking and he says he thinks they are in rats' alley where the dead men lost their bones!

Bash! Crash! Listen to them up there, over-excited, needing a quietening dose of lithium, a soothing rub-down. *Crash! Flash! Summer Lightning.* P.G. Wodehouse and the prize pigs at Blandings, remember? Oh yes, that was a funny one! Wodehouse—another batty old literary man, and a bit of a Nazi too, like Ezra.

•

IT WAS THE SAME WILD weather that woke Louise. She turned over and felt for Max and remembered he was not there.

She was pleased to have finished the Flaubert task, though she was slightly worried about having evaded what Sartre had said on the subject. Now she was planning to take ten or twenty novels by Simenon on her Kindle. That was to be her summer reading, her entertainment. They were usually each a hundred pages long. Simenon was surprisingly consistent about that. Easy writing, easy reading—like the music that was called easy listening. She would read one a day. Reading an article about him in *Libération* had given her a new thought. Simenon had been convinced that he would win the Nobel Prize for literature, and each year, as the announcement approached, he had waited eagerly, and each year had been disappointed, astonished, enraged when he did not get it. Those fools, those idiot bureaucrats in Stockholm, what did they think they were doing, pulling one worthless worm after another out from under stones in the garden of literature? Rabbits out of the Stockholm hat. Who read Marquez or Montale? Who had even heard of Singer or Seifert or Soyinka? And Canetti—he was a cunt, everyone knew that.

It was not his Maigret novels, his *romans policiers*, that Simenon believed deserved these mighty laurels, but the ones that had come to be called his *romans durs*, tough novels, serious stories of real life, of little men who often proved themselves to have strengths that heroes and clever cops lacked.

As the lightning flashed and the thunder cracked overhead,

making her flinch and wince, Louise conceived of what might be her new project. It would combine the pleasure of reading the ever-readable Belgian in his serious mode with an outcome in terms of publication and academic reward. She would reinterpret these works and perhaps understand why he had thought them so important, so deserving and so unfairly discriminated against by the intellectual snobs of the Swedish Academy. Was he right? She would keep an open mind and try to answer that question.

She would also read everything she could find about his life, his two wives, his regular long-term mistresses, his innumerable casual others—whores, chambermaids, casual pick-ups in the streets and corridors of Paris (and he had surely exaggerated the numbers)—to see whether the facts and the books could ever be brought together into some new understanding, some new theory. She amused herself inventing an improbable terminology: Simenonism. A Simenonist.

Another barrage overhead brought Julie scampering to her mother's bed. The little girl climbed in without a word, snuggled up close, and was at once asleep again. It had the effect of bringing renewed sleepiness to Louise.

'Tomorrow . . .' Louise told herself, and was almost asleep when another crash of thunder seemed to shake the whole building and she was awake again, worrying this time about Flaubert. Of course the novel she had edited was famous, honoured, secure. And yet it hadn't always been so. Flaubert himself had once called it 'mediocre'. He'd sent out 150 copies of the first edition to friends and acquaintances and had received acknowledgements from only thirty.

She put her arms lightly around Julie. What a comfort a child could be, especially when they were small. Whatever happened to you beyond the family, they were there, needing you.

•

SYLVIE HAD WOKEN TO THE sound of the storm and in a lull had thought for a moment Bertholdt was weeping beside her. But surely not—he was not a weeper; and no, she listened and he was silent, probably asleep again. Maybe a bad dream. If they had been speaking to one another she would have asked him, but they were not, and it was up to him to break the impasse. He had treated her piggishly, and he would have to apologise. She hated jealousy. And nothing would come of her fantasy fling with Max Jackson. Professor Max. He was a ditherer, held in place by that important wife of his, who had banished him downstairs with the dog while she lived upstairs with Flaubert. Of course it was touching that Max had followed her to the Bastille like that. Just the sight of him there in the foyer, with such haunted, and yet also such *hunting*, eyes . . .

These were drowsy, only half-awake thoughts and in a moment she was asleep again and dreaming. The dream was a half-memory of a moment in a Woody Allen movie about Paris, in which Ernest Hemingway asks Woody (or asks the character who was, so to speak, standing in for Woody) 'Have you ever made love to a truly great woman?' This had seemed so funny at the time, so Hemingway and so silly, that in the dream she laughed, and woke herself up again.

And Bertholdt was not asleep. Out of the darkness came his deep voice. 'You laughed.'

They were speaking again, were they? Did that bare statement, 'You laughed'—did it count? Could it be considered conciliatory? At best, she thought, it was neutral—not the harsh Boche note, but scarcely lyrical or heart-warming.

'I was dreaming.' She said it factually, experimentally, testing the waters.

The waters didn't seem cold.

'It must have been a good one,' he said. 'It sounded cheerful—yes?'

So she reminded him about the Hemingway character's question: 'Have you ever made love to a truly great woman?'

Ah yes. He remembered how she had laughed at that in the movie—'out loud'.

'I did,' she said. 'You didn't laugh, did you, Bertholdt?'

'Yes of course.'

She was silent, as she thought he had been in the cinema.

'Inwardly,' he said.

'You didn't laugh,' she said.

He said, 'I laughed when I was—you know . . . sure.'

'Sure of what? That it was funny?'

There was a flash of lightning and she saw he was sitting up. He said, 'It was funny, Sylvie.' And he laughed as if to illustrate. 'Ha-ha. Ha-ha.'

She yawned. 'I thought it was a hoot.'

'Sometimes humour—it can be . . .'

'What?'

'Well, for example, it can be a question of tone.'

'You make it sound so strenuous.'

He said, very quietly, apologising, 'I don't mean to.'

Silence again, and then, 'I thought I heard you crying,' she said.

'Crying?'

'Weeping—you know. Tears. *Boo-hoo!*'

'No. I do not weep.' When she didn't reply he said, 'Why would I weep?'

In her head she mimicked him: I do not veep. Vy vould I veep? Aloud she said, 'I don't know. Only you can say. Maybe you were thinking about . . . your mother.' She had been going to say 'about your vife', but stopped herself in time.

'My mother is fine.'

'Oh come on, Bertholdt. Isn't there anything that makes you vant to veep—*ever*?'

While they both sat silent there was another flash followed by a thunder crack. 'These are foolish questions,' he said. And then, very gently, 'Would you care to make love, Sylvie?'

'Oh, Bertie.' She was laughing again, rolling from side to side with her hands to her face. But the fact that he'd added her name to the request—called her Sylvie in a special tone—that mysteriously made such a difference. Without the name she might have taken offence. With it, it was funny, but . . . touching. Almost.

'What?' He was puzzled, anxious. 'What is funny?'

She was gasping with laughter. 'You are, Bertholdt.' And then she repeated the Woody joke. 'Have you ever made love to a truly great woman?' and laughed again.

He sat there stiffly, waiting for her to quieten down.

'Come on then,' she said, scrambling across the bed. 'Let's do it.'

6.

FULL OF THE

WARM SOUTH

TWO THOUSAND AND FOURTEEN WAS the first of four years in which Europe and the world beyond would be commemorating the century that had passed since World War I, and the conference Max and Sylvie were cooking up was merely one of many, and insignificant. Such events were happening already, and would go on; but at the same time the world continued to make up and tell its own story in the present tense, as if 100 years ago was of no interest, had scarcely any connection, did not follow on really, obviously, interestingly or in a way that mattered, from what had gone before. There were connections of course, but who knew them and could trace their subtle lines? That was for professionals, academics in their ivory towers. In Syria, Libya, Eritrea—even in Egypt—and always in that remorseless present tense, protest became civil conflict, became civil war, became war. Iraq continued uncorrected, unthankful for the gifts and benefits of Bush and Blair. Afghanistan could not spell itself, or count. And from all these regions refugees spilled like peas across a kitchen floor, to be received into Europe, if they did not die on the way, sometimes with pity and kindness, more often with resistance and rage.

It was not an easy year, nor a convenient one for looking back. The European Union was in conflict with itself, unemployment was high, Spain's economy, and Portugal's, were weak, Greece was bankrupt, while Germany opened doors but demanded austerity for all. And so it went on—the world telling its own story in action, in full colour, getting on with the *now* of everything, on the news and on the worldwide web, even as it was asked to look back and retell that old black-and-white one of mud and blood, rifle and bayonet, trenches and no man's land—of going over the top and of thousands dead in a day.

Against this background, what did one memorable Midsummer Night dinner at Le Procope and its decisions signify? Not much more than another university seminar, a junket, a paper-chase, a chance for some to strut and fret their twenty minutes on a stage and then (probably) be heard no more. It meant literature, which meant almost nothing in the bigger picture, and almost everything to those oddballs for whom life was meaningless and ugly without it.

•

MAX WAS COMING BACK FROM a solo breakfast at the café on the Place Saint-Sulpice, with a few supplies and a baguette that were to be his lunch, when he came upon Helen White in the narrow street outside the big black gate to his courtyard. She saw him, turned away as if to escape (the small scuttling animal again), then changed her mind and turned back to face him. She was carrying a large flat bag, in shape rather like the one she'd brought on their picnic, but this was plain white canvas—no yellow stripes. So she was looking for him—must be. What else?—how odd—and (he decided after a moment's apprehension) how nice.

'Welcome,' he said.

'Am I?'

'Welcome? Of course.'

And, as if to show she was, he did the regulation cheek kissing—*mwa*, *mwa*, and even a third. *Mwa.*

'I thought . . .' she said, and then seemed unsure what she thought.

'Come in.' He flashed his key at the black barrier that he thought of sometimes as the Great Gate of Kiev, which clicked its tongue—as if this matter of getting through it was nothing—and unlatched itself.

'I brought you . . .' she began, stepping inside.

He prompted her. 'You brought me something?'

She patted the big bag. 'Something to look at, that's all.'

'Excellent. Let's look then.'

He led her indoors, put away the things he was carrying. 'Have you had breakfast?'

Yes, no, she thought so, wasn't hungry.

'Cup of coffee—instant? Or tea?'

'Tea would be nice, thanks.' So it was English breakfast tea, which he made in a pot. He poured himself one too, and put half the baguette, a block of cheese and a knife on a plate, all in easy reach, telling her to help herself. She was sitting at the table already, sliding out from her bag two broad sketchbooks. The first she opened at a page of drawings and watercolours of leaves—

many leaves. Each was single, sometimes attached to branch or twig, others just lying where they had fallen or been placed. They were varieties of green, from palest to very dark.

'These are lovely,' he said.

She turned a page, and then another. More green leaves. 'Beautiful,' he said.

He was puzzled, interested, with a slight feeling of anxiety; and pleased he could think of no reason why he should not be having this encounter—this visit. No need to turn her away—and no wish to either.

'The colours are so delicate,' he said.

'These are spring and summer leaves,' she said. 'Good for poets but not the best season for painters.'

'But you have others.'

Yes she had others. The second folder was autumn and winter— and here were all the shades, from green as it tended and faded towards yellow, or flared into orange and red, or died into brown. This, she said, was her 'Margaret, are you grieving?' sketchbook.

'Ah yes indeed,' he said, taking his time, poring over them, slowly turning the pages, murmuring the lines of Gerard Manley Hopkins.

> Margaret, are you grieving
> Over Goldengrove unleaving . . .

The leaves were many shapes and sizes, and with differing patterns—from one colour to many, and from smooth surfaces to stippled and spotted, pimpled and pricked.

'So you're an artist,' he said. 'I thought of you as a word person.'

'I think I'm both,' she said.

'I think you are. It was nice of you to bring them. Thank you.'

And then, because that might have seemed a signal to terminate the visit, which was not what he wanted, he said, 'There's such a talent here.'

And there was—precision, delicacy, sense of colours and ability to mix them, with a resulting (what else could you call it?) beauty. 'Do you paint other things? Whole branches? Trees? What about flowers? People?'

'I think I'm a specialist,' she said. And then, 'Like Morandi.'

'Of course. The bottles.'

'I thought . . .' She looked up at him, and began again. 'Coming here—I thought it was better than cutting off my ear and sending that.'

'Much better,' he said. He thought he had allowed no trace of alarm into the reply; but he had not forgotten the lithium, the description of herself as 'mad'. He said, 'I hope you didn't seriously think of that, did you?'

'Only in fun.'

Was that reassuring, or ambiguous? He imagined the ear arriving in a parcel with a message saying, 'Love, Vincent—(just joking!)'

'Much too nice an ear to be sacrificed,' he said.

'Thank you, Max.'

And then, smiling down at the floor, she said, 'I keep baring my ankle and you don't look.'

He looked now. She had a small owl tattoo, like the one he'd had done that night with her. He pulled his trouser leg up and held his ankle beside hers. They matched exactly.

'A memento,' she said.

'Indeed,' he said. 'Well done!'

•

THE VILLA CARLEONE, WHICH THREE branches of Louise's extended family kept and shared for holidays, was on the Golfo Paradiso, not more than twenty kilometres east of Genoa. It was expensive to keep and to run, but the clan, all affluent, shared the costs so they were able to have a permanent housekeeper whose husband was the gardener. These two, Adriana and Bruno, a couple in their early sixties, lived in the house throughout the year. When summer came around, or at other times of the year when some or all of the family chose to be on vacation there, the housekeeper could also be the cook, and the gardener was the chauffeur. Sometimes the branches of the family took turns to occupy it solo; at others they shared. There were rivalries and competition among the cousins, but mostly they liked one another. Among the adults there had been the dispute over the grandfathers' wills, and now there was tension between Uncle Henri's second wife and his daughters to his first; but occupations were arranged to avoid internecine warfare and fratricidal overlaps. The villa was by general agreement a zone of neutrality and peace.

The house was on three floors, with balconies at the front looking out over and through pines to the Mediterranean. A garden with gravelled zig-zag paths led down through the pines and cactus plants to the rocks and the sea. There was a boat-shed and a sailing dinghy, which Bruno kept at anchor, or in rough weather pulled up a ramp into the shed. In calm weather the children, and swimmers among the adults, bathed there and lay on the flat rocks in the sun. When the seas came up rough and broke against and over the rocks, Bruno closed off the paths and access was forbidden; but they could troop down as a group for swimming, through the village to a more sheltered bay where the stones clattered as the waves beat in, and rattled as they withdrew.

There were night lights in the pines, turned on by Bruno at

sundown, which was also the moment when the bats appeared, so hard at work and so mysteriously noiseless in flight. They were hunting an invisible prey, also in flight. It was war in the air but, unlike the daylight warfare waged by swallows, it took place in silence. The sky, as night came on, took on a velvet texture, without quite losing the colour blue, with clouds still white and the moon rising yellow among them.

There was a *passeggiata*—a paved pathway below the coast road that offered walks in either direction, over the rocks, sometimes along clifftops and through fishing villages, with small swimming beaches at intervals. And above the same coast road there were steep paths climbing into the foothills of the Ligurian mountains.

Along that coast were resorts like Rapallo and Portofino, the Cinque Terre and La Spezia; and it had a history which Max and Louise knew and relished. Shelley (with a copy of Keats in his pocket) had been drowned there, his yacht wrecked in a sudden storm. His friends Byron and Trelawney had cremated his body on the beach. Inland from Viareggio, Puccini had lived and written his operas. Ezra Pound had lived at Rapallo and broadcast in support of Mussolini during World War II. Branded a traitor, he had spent weeks in a wire cage in the American army's detention camp near Pisa, and written some of his best-known poems there.

So you could think of it in a way as a wild place, a place for one kind or another of wildness. But Max had thought of it always in terms of summer, vacation time, of the Keats line 'O for a beaker full of the warm south'. For him, Genoa and that coast were the warm south.

Every year since their marriage he had been there with Louise—2014 was the first time she had gone without him, taking the children as usual, and Skipper. This—like his removal downstairs—had been by agreement. It was called a trial separation. Max was sorry not to be there. He loved the place, and loved being there with the children. But he was also enjoying his freedom. Sometimes he felt endangered by it, as if he were suddenly weightless and might fly off into space; at others there was the feeling that it was right—'time to move on'. But move on where? England? New Zealand? Or just here in Paris, but without Louise?

He was still anchored to her—by Jean-Claude and Julie, by their past, their youth, their years together. Even now they communicated almost daily by Skype. She reported on Simenon, who was not, she said, shaping up to be one who should have had the Nobel Prize. She was entertained, or perhaps more precisely (she said, correcting herself) *engaged*, by Simenon, but without being seriously impressed. In fact, she preferred his *policiers* to the *romans durs* he had rated so highly.

She'd had her Flaubert text back from Gallimard, copy-edited. Proofs would come next and would be sent to her Paris address.

Max in turn told her about his progress with the book on Naipaul and Lessing. It was a good subject and he was pleased with progress.

There was news from her about the children, the local village, the inexhaustible city of Genoa, which claimed the Blessed Virgin as its queen; and from him about their neighbourhood and the currently somnolent Sorbonne Nouvelle. But he edited what he told her: nothing about quicksilver Sylvie; nor about his right ankle and the owl inscribed there; nor about Helen White, who even now was showing him her skill in painting leaves.

•

MAX AND HELEN'S MORNING PASSED effortlessly and they had a scratch lunch together, opening tins, making toast, trying and then rejecting a new cheese he'd bought that morning. He told her about his work on Naipaul and Lessing, and about the effort that had gone into Louise's edition of *L'Éducation Sentimentale*. She risked telling him her joke about *Flaubert's Parrot* and he laughed. She talked about Edward Thomas, and how much she would like to be part of the First World War *journée d'études* he and Sylvie were planning. Finally it seemed there was no way of protracting the visit further and she gathered her things together, the two sketchbooks, her wallet, her cell phone, the capacious carry-all, the light raincoat she'd been wearing. He went with her to the door, where she opened it ahead of him and turned back, holding out a hand to be shaken.

'Au revoir, Max,' she said, and he said, 'Au revoir.'

They had been getting on so well, enjoying one another's company, so a question hovered in the air between them, until she said rather hurriedly, running the words together, 'I'd been wondering what you'd have said if I'd suggested a massage.'

'Me too,' he said.

'You mean . . . wondering?'

'Yes.'

'Well—I suppose we'll never know.'

'Not unless you do.'

'Do what?'

'Suggest it.'

'That sounds . . . hopeful?'

'I was hopeful, yes.'

'Shall we?'

'Why not?' And he reached past her and pushed the door shut. 'Come.'

In his bedroom, with the curtains drawn, he took off his shoes and stripped to the waist. She shed shoes and some clothing. It took a while, but soon the magic of those fingers, those strong hands on his back, was working.

'You need to take off this belt,' she said.

He took it off, and the trousers with it. As he did this, she too removed her trousers. 'For freer movement,' she said.

He admired her ankle owl, and kissed it—a quick peck. 'Where did you have this done?'

'Same place, same guy. I went back. He remembered us.'

On his stomach again Max adjusted himself to accommodate an erection.

Her hands ranged further—down his back, his lower spine, over his buttocks and to his inner thighs. Encountering no resistance she explored further, and found the penis.

'That's a rock,' she said.

'So hard it hurts.'

'Shouldn't we give it some relief?'

They were shedding the last of their clothes now. 'Should have a condom,' he said, swallowing and choking on the words, not sounding as if he meant it or it mattered. This, and all his thoughts now, were like flies in an empty kitchen on a hot summer's day. They buzzed and flickered and came to sudden stops, surprising silences.

They made love, slowly at first, relishing, spinning it out, making the most of it. And then, as if at a signal, it became violent. The bed rocked and shuddered, the bed-head banged against the wall. Helen let out chirps and chirrups, and he saw that her eyes were weirdly rolled back and her eyelids flickering, fast. The sounds concentrated into a sort of shout, two shouts, not protracted but briefly loud, his and hers, diminishing into a series of exclamations of the '*Oh my God!*', '*Oh Jesus!*' sort, as if they had been acting in a bad movie. Sex was a cliché, but who cared if it could be so nice, so entirely satisfactory?

He slept a while, and when he woke she was up on one elbow, looking at him.

'Did you imagine you were fucking Sylvie?' she said.

'No.'

'Louise?'

'No.'

'Who?'

'Who what?'

'Were you fucking? Who did you think it was?'

'You. I imagined I was fucking *you*.' She still looked into his eyes. 'Helen,' he said. 'I thought it was Helen White. That one.'

'And you were. You fucking *were*.'

'I fucking was, wasn't I?'

They were quiet a while, and then he asked, 'What about you?'

'What?'

'Was I the boyfriend? What's his name? Hugh? Was I Hugh for you?'

'No you weren't Hugh. You were you.'

She said this very fast, and they laughed again, and it occurred to him that this was such an English-language conversation. There must be an equivalent you could have in French but he wasn't sure what the nouns would be, which verbs, how it would go.

He dozed a moment, a few minutes, and woke worrying. He said, 'About the ear . . .'

'What ear?'

'The one you were going to cut off and send me.'

'Oh that one.' She put a hand to it, as if she knew which one.

'It was a joke—wasn't it?'

112

She propped again to look at him. 'Everything's a joke.'

He tried to say 'No it's not' but she kept going.

'The world and all the men and women merely players. And one man in his time cuts off many parts. A joke, Max. The moon and sun and stars—they're kept in their orbits by lithium. Shakespeare says so. Or he would have if he'd known . . .'

'You're babbling,' he said.

'Yes, do you mind?'

He laughed and kissed her, and threw himself back with both hands behind his head. No he didn't mind. A moment later he was putting the worry to rest again, between her legs.

It was mid afternoon and he was showered and dressed when someone knocked. Helen was brushing her hair in the bedroom and was ready to leave. She had told him she was going home to Norfolk for a few weeks of the summer break, leaving tomorrow. He supposed this might mean they would have to say goodbye in a different way now. Did one fuck, or two, or whatever way you counted what they'd done together, make them lovers?

It was the concierge at the door. A parcel had come for Madame. Monsieur Ferney knew she was away so thought it best to deliver it here. Max thanked him and brought it in.

It had come from Gallimard, Louise's proofs, and it occurred to Max that he could take them upstairs at once; that he could show Helen the apartment up there, their library, the office which had once been shared and was now all Louise's, the roof garden, 'the picture' . . . It would be 'a nice thing to do'—a little farewell gift—but not only for her. It would be a gift to himself as well. That was how he thought of it at that moment. He relished the thought of her seeing these things, sharing the ambience of his life as it had been.

'Come,' he said. 'We'll deliver this upstairs.'

Her face showed surprise—but eagerness too. She was already carrying the raincoat and had the carry-all with the sketchbooks over her shoulder.

So they went up in the little iron cage lift, which moved slowly enough for kissing, but this was a lipsticky one, and brief. He wondered how long it had been since he had kissed Louise in there, and 'deranged' her hair. Upstairs, they went first to the office and put the proofs down on the desk.

'Louise and I used to share this,' he said. 'A desk each—and the filing cabinets.'

'And now . . .'

'All hers.'

'That's not fair.'

'What is fair? It's convenient.' It was not entirely convenient, so he added, 'Inevitable. Unavoidable.'

Helen strolled about from room to room, browsing bookshelves, admiring the views and the roof garden, checking Jean-Claude's and Julie's rooms and how (boy/girl) they differed; and while this went on Max opened the parcel of proofs, looked them over, checked, against his memory of Louise's print-out, what changes had been made so he could report to her next time they Skyped.

Helen was interested in the kitchen, in the bathrooms, and (more) in Louise's clothes. But what she kept coming back to was 'the picture'.

She called to Max, 'This is Cézanne.'

He came to the door of the room. 'We call it "the picture",' he said. 'We never allow ourselves to name the painter or the title he gave the work.'

'He called it the pond of the sisters,' Helen said. 'I've seen this painting. It's in the Courtauld Institute.' When he didn't reply she said, 'In London. Somerset House.'

He nodded. 'Yes, indeed.'

'So what is it, Max?' She looked closely. 'That's oil on canvas. It's not a print.'

'You think it's a fake?'

She was still up close, considering. 'It looks awfully—'

'Good?'

'Real.'

Max said, 'You mean authentic. Yes it does, because it is. Cézanne had two shots at that painting before he did the one you've seen in the Courtauld.'

'So this is . . .'

'That's "the picture".'

'"The picture". My God, it must be worth . . .'

'We don't talk about that.'

'If there's to be a divorce . . .'

He must have known what she meant, what her mind had leapt to—that it would have to be sold and the money divided—but he shut down on it. 'I don't think so, Helen.' Naming her was in effect firm, custodial, even admonitory. He would not go there. Was it the divorce he would not discuss, or the settlement, the distribution of assets? Helen couldn't be sure and probably neither could he.

'Time to go,' he said.

He went back to the office and arranged the proofs neatly over the desk, so they were ready for Louise when she returned.

Out in the vestibule he called to Helen and tapped the numbers of the security code into the alarm. She came, clutching the carry-all over her shoulder, wearing the raincoat loosely over that. 'It's raining out there,' she said. She was ready for the street.

The lift was silent as they descended and they did not kiss.

Downstairs he embraced her briefly, formally, properly. If

Monsieur Ferney had looked out from his lodge and seen it, it would have made no impression. It was as if 'the picture', or her mention of it and of a possible divorce, had put a small barrier between them; had brought a minor cold snap to their weather.

'Au revoir, Helen.'

'Adieu, Max.'

Adieu? Did she mean it? Or was it just an English mistake in French? And she seemed in a hurry to get away. He was still asking himself this question as he watched her pass through the courtyard and the big black gate, which unlocked itself when approached from the garden, and out into the street.

•

MAX KEPT UP WITH WHAT was happening in New Zealand by checking the newspapers online. There was never much news, or not much of importance away from where it was happening, and he tried not to waste time on it; but he did not want to lose touch altogether. It was not just loyalty; it was fear, as if New Zealand was an anchor that kept him from floating off into abstraction. He was not entirely sure what this meant, but he had known, when he said it to Louise, that it was something important.

So, when a five-year-old boy called Jack Dixon was swept away and drowned at Mount Maunganui just after his grandmother had photographed him, Max read about it on *The New Zealand Herald* website, and about the unsuccessful search for the body that went on for many days. It was winter there, so the seas could be wild. He looked at the photograph of the blond, smiling boy, and thought of his own children. He knew what every New Zealander knew, that the west coast was the wild one, the danger zone, where you swam only between the flags if you swam at all, and where, even so, numbers drowned every year. The east coast was the benign one; the safe beaches were there. But that was the trap; because now and then, and especially in winter, some parts of that coast could produce bad storms, and worse, what were called 'freak' waves that were 'out of character' and out to get you. They took people by surprise—took them, as the taniwha of Māori legend did, and drowned them. Mount Maunganui was an eastern beach. It should have been safe. Usually it was. This, young Jack's death, should not have happened. No one was to blame. There had been no carelessness. The taniwha had struck, that was all. It had reached out and taken Jack away, not to be returned alive, possibly never to be found.

Max's mind roamed free. He thought about Helen, and wondered why she had said 'Adieu' rather than 'Au revoir'. 'Adieu' was dramatic; it was worse, melodramatic—a sort of romantic, 'Goodbye forever'. He thought of Sylvie, and felt he was in love with her, and was confused. He talked to Louise, face-to-face via a jerky Skype connection, and felt pleased they had talked, with so much space, so many kilometres, between them. He talked to Jean-Claude, then to Julie, and told them he loved them to bits, and did, and warned them to be careful in the sea. He thought of Julien, and exchanged emails with him that were refreshingly relaxed and relatively improper. He thought of his sister in New Zealand and, remembering their childhood together, drafted her a long message, and deleted it.

And then, like a counterweight sometimes, at night came images or thoughts of young Jack. The body had not been found and the *Herald* was reporting that every day his father scanned and combed that long beach that ran east from Mount Maunganui all the way to Opotiki, searching. It was Max's thought, half thought half dream, that brought an image of the drowned boy merging into the plan for a conference about the poets killed in 'the War to end Wars', and then the poem Kipling had written about his son who had died in it:

'Have you news of my boy Jack?'
  Not this tide.
'When d'you think that he'll come back?'
  Not with this wind blowing, and this tide.

III.

TOWARDS

AUTUMN

7.

A CASE FOR

MAIGRET?

IT WAS THE DAY GINA had chosen for the big cleaning job. She took it very seriously, applied herself vigorously, wanting her work to be noticed, admired and approved. She had done the two bathrooms and the kitchen, the children's bedrooms, and the one that had been Monsieur-and-Madame's together and was now mysteriously (and sadly, Gina thought) only Madame's. Now she was in the principal sitting room, using her feather duster, knocking the horrible male nudes this way and that, when she arrived at the centrepiece, which always received special attention. The space was vacant, unoccupied. Where 'the picture'—the important one—had been, there was only a gap.

Gina did not know anything about this painting except that it was always referred to with a kind of reverence which she was quick enough to notice and respect. She had never enquired about it—only took her tone about it, and her treatment of it, from Monsieur and Madame. As a painting she had always thought of it as sinister—a green landscape with large trees casting shadows over a dark pond that made her feel, though there were no human figures, someone must have drowned there. To Georges she referred to it as 'the scary one'. But Madame was so serious about it, Gina had told Georges it must be worth a lot of money. No one would talk like that, in that hushed voice, about a picture if it wasn't worth a mint.

So Gina arrived at its place on the wall, and its absence, with shock and surprise. How had she failed until this moment to see that it wasn't there? She must have had her attention taken up with the work, item by item.

She saw that the two hooks were still in place. It would have been removed very easily, lifted off them—and in fact there had been times in the past when she'd seen it taken off the wall and set down somewhere—which must surely be what had happened now. No one unauthorised could get in here. There was the alarm, to which she and Monsieur Ferney, and no one else outside the family, had the code.

She thought about what this absence might mean, and then stopped thinking about it and went on with her work. Something must be afoot, and in time she would hear about it. Downstairs she knocked at Monsieur Jackson's door just to check with him that it was right. There was no answer. She thought of telling the concierge and then decided she would not give him the opportunity to be the important one, the one who knew everything, telling her either that it didn't matter, or that it did and she was foolish not to have told him sooner.

Later that day she mentioned it to Georges. She supposed 'the picture' must have been taken down by Madame—but for what?

Restoration work, Georges thought; that was what happened to pictures in the Louvre. Old work was taken down to be cleaned and restored.

But it worried her, and she worried Georges about it. It couldn't have been stolen, could it? So after all Monsieur Ferney, concierge and therefore ruler of that roost, had to be approached.

His first response was defensive—as if he had been blamed. He assured Georges and Gina that no one unusual or suspicious-looking had come by; the security had not been breached. But he was anxious too, and surprisingly uncertain what they should do next. Max had not returned and it was getting on towards evening.

They discussed it in below-stairs tones, almost collaboratively, as if the behaviour of their betters was always mysterious and faintly absurd. You could never be sure whether you would be rebuked for doing something unnecessary, or for not doing something necessary. That was the question. To warn or not to warn?

Monsieur Ferney decided they should act. He would put it in the form of an enquiry. Was it right that 'the picture' was not in its usual place on the wall; or was it wrong? And if it was not right, what should they do? He would of course make the call himself.

Even on the phone, and in her role as their employer, 'Madame' could not conceal her alarm. Where was Max, she demanded?

Monsieur Ferney told her Monsieur Jackson had not come home yet.

They must tell him to call her at once—and they should call the police. Meanwhile she would make arrangements for her own return at the earliest possible moment.

Half an hour later she rang to say she had secured a flight, Air France, Genoa to Charles de Gaulle, direct. It left at 17.40 and arrived at 19.10. She would be with them that evening. The children would remain there with their aunt and cousins.

They were able to tell her that Max had been called and was on his way home—would be there any minute. And the police had been called and had told them not to disturb anything that might be evidence.

•

LOUISE'S FIRST INTERVIEW WITH THE police officer, an ordinary cop who came to the apartment late that evening, was unsatisfactory. And Max seemed helpless—stunned and disbelieving, as she was, but with nothing useful to offer. She wondered in passing whether it was an effect of being banished downstairs. She had always been able to depend on him in a crisis, but not now, not any more.

And she was herself too distracted, too distressed, feeling that at any moment hysteria might take hold of her, to think much about her husband, though she did question him. Yes, he had been up to the apartment while she was away, but he thought only once, to lay out the Flaubert proofs ready for her return. And no, he could not say for sure that 'the picture' had been there. He felt pretty sure that it must have been or he would surely have noticed the gap. His problem was (he said) that he had no precise memory of having seen it—so could not help with pinpointing when the theft had occurred.

The cop was not stupid. He had heard of Cézanne, knew he was famous, and did not understand why a work by such a great painter had not been a matter of public knowledge. Louise thought he was suspicious that this might be a case of insurance fraud rather than burglary. She could see he thought she was not being straight with him, that she was being evasive—which was not correct, but there was a lot that was unusual and difficult to explain in a few sentences.

Louise asked to speak to his senior officer.

He said there was no need for that; the matter was already being passed on to the 'Brigade against the Traffic in Cultural Goods', which had its offices in Trente-Six, police headquarters on the Quai des Orfèvres. An appointment would be made for her there and she could tell her story to the experts. Meanwhile, the apartment was being carefully inspected and checked for fingerprints and other relevant evidence.

The concierge, along with the *femme de ménage* and her husband, were being questioned separately and together. For the moment that was all that could be done. The photographer and the person checking for prints would be finished very soon.

He thanked Madame, and wished her good night.

•

HELEN WHITE WAS AT HOME in England at the Norfolk mill-house her parents had turned into a sort of retirement retreat. She had just had a talk with her mother about her life in Paris. She was enjoying it, she said, and it was rewarding. She felt well there and was being conscientious about her medication. Her French was improving every day, the courses she was taking were fascinating, there was an interesting professor, Max Jackson, a poet, who had become a friend . . . and so on. Her interest in Gurdjieff (and in Zen too) continued, and no, she did not allow their 'hocus-pocus' (her mother did not approve) to stand in the way of science and medicine. They were complementary, not opposing, disciplines.

She had tried to say the things a mother wants to hear. These were not untruths, just incomplete. Edited. In her life, she found (and she supposed it was the same for everyone) editing was necessary.

And now she was sitting in a punt under willows reading *The Zone of Interest*, the new Amis novel. She had twice stopped reading it, and then been drawn back to go on, laughing out loud sometimes, sometimes throwing it down in anger or disgust, but never overboard into the stream—and then drawn back to it by something in the prose. Yes, the prose; but the story too. She wanted to know what happened next.

She had begun because Max (all detailed and serious thought of whom she had forbidden herself for the moment) had talked about it. Not that he had recommended it. In fact he'd said things that might have been meant to put her off; to suggest that her 'precarious' mind might over-react to the horrors. Something about lithium—that she might (but laughing—or anyway smiling) need a 'double dose' before embarking on it. Yet when she'd asked to borrow it he had not said no. And she didn't feel unsettled by it—not in that way, not schizoid—just annoyed . . .

The rhyming accident interrupted her thought, detained her, and she had to linger on it—

Not schizoid. Just annoyed.

But what annoyed her was that Amis had put such a gripping and funny story in such a horrible place. It was like putting a Walt Disney kids' movie about cute animals in a slaughterhouse.

She laughed at this thought, and then told herself she was as bad as Amis—if he was bad. Couldn't anything be funny, anything at all, if you wanted it to be? It didn't mean it was always and for all time funny: only for the moment of the joke—after which life went on and you went back to being calm and serious. Jokes were an interruption to the normal order of things, and Amis, like Dickens, made such good ones.

Maybe it would have been OK if he hadn't written that serious essay and put it at the end of the book, explaining the novel and its worthy purpose. And then, after the essay, there were the dedications—even one to his Jewish mother-in-law and his two (consequently) Jewish daughters.

Max had said Amis-the-younger was always kicked in the backside whatever he did; and he had never won the Booker Prize. It was something about his brilliance, Max said—the kind people felt annoyed by and free to lay in to. In that essay you could feel Amis preparing himself for the kicks, asking that they be not too hard because he was a good boy, *really*.

But Helen thought the dedication deserved one. She was standing in the punt now, punishing the younger Amis, kicking him, kicking the side rail. 'Take that, Amis. And that, and *that*!' The punt rocked and she tottered and fell back into her seat.

A moorhen, alarmed, swam out from the bank, followed by a little line of jet-black chicks. Life was very good. The willows, green and trailing in the waters of the millrace, were beautiful; so were the reflections; and the purple wildflowers, and the green and gold reeds, visited by delicate turquoise damselflies.

Willows and wildflowers: so many Ws—two to each noun. Margaret was not grieving and nor was Goldengrove un-leaving. And Helen was not thinking about Max. That was an achievement. She gave herself high marks for that. No Margaret, no Max, only willows and wildflowers. Hooray!

•

A DAY PASSED AND THEN it was time for Louise's appointment at Trente-Six. She was kept waiting there; but when the specialist officer arrived, very civil and spruce in his uniform, he apologised, introduced himself as Captain Olivier, led her to the lifts and upstairs, showed her into a pleasant office with a view of the river. He offered her coffee. She accepted, and as it was being brought he explained that he had taken a few extra minutes to check on Cézanne thefts and forgeries. 'I understand, Madame, that the painting missing from your apartment was a Cézanne.'

'It was,' she said. 'It is a version of *L'Étang des Sœurs*.'

'I see—interesting. Painted with the knife?'

'Yes—I believe so.' She was not certain but did not say so. 'But you won't find this one listed in the usual catalogues and inventories.'

'I don't understand, Madame. There is a reason?'

'Because the family has never had it authenticated.'

She recognised his change of expression. He was not going to take her entirely seriously. Perhaps he'd decided to treat her with respect, because she was who she was, a senior professor at the Sorbonne Nouvelle; but, as far as he was concerned at this moment, there was no Cézanne. There was a painting—he would accept that, and that it was gone, apparently stolen; but it was unlikely it had been painted by Paul Cézanne.

He handed her the coffee with special politeness. She declined sugar and the offer of a biscuit.

'I understand your position, Captain Olivier,' she said. 'Your doubt. But I and the family have no doubt. There has never been any. Among us the facts are well known. The story was passed down through the family and it never changed. It is documented in letters, which we have kept. My great-grandfather was an early admirer of Cézanne, and this painting was a version of the work currently held in a London gallery. Cézanne was not satisfied and did the same scene again, I believe twice, enlarging it each time. My forebear admired the first attempt and bought it. It was sold, as painters have always done, to a friend for what even at the time was a reduced price.'

'If the story as it has come to you can be confirmed, then this is a work possibly worth a very large sum.'

'Very large—yes, undoubtedly.'

'Yet you have never had it authenticated or valued.'

'No, never.'

'Why is that, Madame?'

Louise explained. 'We have never had any reason to doubt the story. It may have made its way into some of the biographies—I believe it has in at least one. There was no need for authentication, and the idea has always been avoided. A painting known to be worth so much would be an inconvenience. It would have attracted attention and interest, experts would have wanted to look at it and write about it, it would have been vulnerable to theft, and would have needed insurance and security at a level none of us would have wanted to pay for. I don't believe we could have kept it at home and had the pleasure of it there every day, to be looked at and appreciated. We were happy to quarrel among ourselves about ownership—and there has been one court case over it, in which its value was set at a notional five hundred thousand euros—enough to explain the quarrel without acknowledging what we all knew: that it was worth so much more.'

'I see.' He was taking notes. 'You have a photograph of it?'

'Yes,' she said. 'Of course.' She handed it to him across the desk. 'It's not a very good image, I'm afraid. I'm sure there are others— possibly lodged with our lawyers at the time the matter went to court.' She hoped this was true, but was not sure.

Still looking at the photograph, he said, 'I will need to see those as soon as possible, Madame. And copies of those family documents, please.'

He looked up. 'Yes it is certainly *L'Étang des Sœurs*—or a copy.'

'It is not a copy, Captain Olivier.'

He completed his notes and closed the page. He was perhaps not as sceptical as he had been at first, but not convinced either.

She asked, 'How do you proceed from here, Monsieur?'

'The scene of the theft has been examined for evidence. We will work on authentication—and of course it's a great pity this has not been done long ago by experts. And then if the scene examination offers nothing that we can act upon immediately, we wait.'

'Yes, I see. What do you wait for?'

'If we are lucky there is a ransom demand. Of course, if this were an already well-known work, acknowledged by experts, the demand would be very large. In this case . . .' He shrugged. 'We shall see. But you know, Madame, sometimes works are stolen, not so much for profit as for ownership.'

'I understand that perfectly, Captain. And I think that is the case now. There will not be a ransom demand.'

'Why do you say that, Madame?'

'Because I believe I know who has stolen it.'

He leaned forward over the desk. 'Explain, please.'

Louise took a small sheaf of notes out of her handbag. 'These are the people I suspect. They are my relatives.'

'Ah, I see.' His eyebrows were raised. Perhaps he was only surprised, but she thought sceptical too, and perhaps amused.

She explained about the disputed bequest, the painting and the family château. 'My guess is it will be somewhere in the recesses of the château—well hidden. You will have to conduct a search.'

'Madame Professor,' he said, giving her title its full weight, 'we would have to have a reason for that. Your suspicion would not be enough. There would need to be some evidence. Of course if we found a fingerprint or DNA . . .'

Louise wondered about DNA evidence in families, and how closely they went to matching. 'I've told you what I believe,' she said. 'I cannot do more.'

'Thank you. We will do our best, I assure you.'

All at once she surprised herself by weeping.

'I'm sorry,' she said.

'Don't apologise, Madame. I understand.'

'I think they have it and I will never see it again.'

She should not have said that. It was indeed what she felt, but saying so made it more difficult to stop the tears.

His hand hesitated towards her, as if his thought were of patting her somewhere—the shoulder perhaps, or the arm—but he was unsure that would be right, or appreciated. 'Let us hope,' he said, as the hand hung in the air, awaiting instructions, 'that there will be good evidence. People, when they are not professional criminals—they make mistakes.'

Through her inconvenient tears she noticed how he rated professionals above amateurs, even in crime. 'My relatives are clever people,' she said.

'Of course.'

'Where money and ownership are concerned, they don't make mistakes.'

'I will keep that in mind. But you understand, Madame, before we can proceed in any way against the people on your list, we need some evidence.'

'That will be difficult, I'm sure. Someone will have been employed.' She smiled. 'A professional.'

He made more notes, or perhaps was only crossing t's and dotting i's while Louise rallied herself, and sat up straight in her chair. Some part of her brain was entertained by the thought that life imitated art, and that she had a part in a small drama that might have been drafted by Flaubert.

Captain Olivier was looking at her keenly. He seemed to hover on the brink of something, and then to take the plunge. 'Your husband occupies the downstairs apartment.'

'He does.'

'And—excuse the enquiry, but I do need to understand . . .'

'Of course.'

'Is this some kind of formal separation?'

She wondered whether she should tell him it was not his business; but she was curious to know what was in his mind. 'It is not yet formal,' she said, 'but possibly heading towards something of the kind.'

'So a divorce is not absolutely out of the question?'

She did not like the question, but she answered. 'Not absolutely, no.'

'In which case there would be a division of assets?'

She saw what he was suggesting, that Max might have made a pre-emptive strike on the family's most valuable transportable asset. It was a clever thought and, though she dismissed it, she found it interesting that it was where an experienced police officer's mind went. Simenon would have followed him there.

'Please understand, Madame,' Captain Olivier was saying, 'my position is this: I begin by knowing nothing, and I have to try to learn, and from what I learn to understand. I have to test the waters.'

She wanted to say that Max would not have stolen the painting, she was sure of that, but since it had not been frankly suggested it could not be frankly denied. And why should the idea not be entertained? It made the whole thing more interesting. There had always been a lawless streak in Max—something that went with the poet, and which she'd thought, at least until recently, like the poet, had been left behind.

'You have to do your job,' she said.

He nodded, and made a note. 'Thank you, Madame, you have been most helpful—and understanding.'

•

MAX AND JULIEN HAD LUNCH at La Grande Mosquée near the Sorbonne Nouvelle. Julien, who liked to give offence in private to public morals and institutions, invented labels for this restaurant: '*Terrorism with Taste*', for example, or '*Isis it Ain't*'.

There was something raffish and insouciant about Julien which Max found disarming and amusing. It made their colleagues (especially Louise) impatient; but to Max it was a relief from the propriety that ruled the Sorbonne Nouvelle. At La Mosquée they liked the Arab food and Arab ambience, the bead curtains, colourful cushions and rugs, the cedar-wood and fretwork partitions and tiled floors; and the courtyard where you could sit and eat pastries or sugary cakes and drink mint tea under trees, while locals who came, or whose parents had come, from Morocco, Tunisia, Algeria, smoked their hookahs.

Max had replied yes to the lunch invitation and said there was something serious he wanted to talk about; and now he was spilling it all out, the whole embarrassing, difficult 'thing' he found himself in: how he had taken his student-friend Helen White to the upstairs apartment and now 'the picture' was missing.

Julien knew about 'the picture'—had visited, had seen it in the days before the marital severance. 'You're not saying she took it?' And when Max didn't reply, 'Are you?'

'I can't be sure,' Max said. 'That's what makes it so difficult. It was there—she and I were there. We looked at it, talked about it. She loved it of course. And she had a big carry-all sort of canvas bag for her sketchbooks. It could have gone in there when I was in the office with the proofs. But on the other hand I suppose it's just as possible someone else stole it.'

'Who? Why?'

'Thieves. For its value. For money. Or Louise's family. There's been a long-running dispute about it.'

'What do you think?'

'Both seem—well . . . unlikely,' Max said.

'An almighty coincidence,' Julien said. 'What does she say?'

'Helen? She says nothing. I haven't been able to track her down. She was off next day to her family in England and I don't have an address.'

'Email?'

'Not responding. I'm not even sure the email I have is current.'

'Why was she there?'

'I told you—she called to show me her artwork.'

Julien was amused. 'Her etchings?'

'Watercolours,' Max said. 'Of leaves.'

'Leaves. Fascinating.'

'Spring and autumn leaves. Green and gold.'

'Nice,' Julien said.

Max tried again. 'While she was visiting downstairs a parcel came for Louise—a set of proofs. I took them upstairs and Helen came with me—'

He stopped explaining because he could see that Julien did not think the important question was being answered. Why had Helen been there with him, in the upstairs apartment? Max had asked himself the same question. Why had he invited her? There had been a thought of somehow gathering her into his life; including her. It had been a generous impulse, the immediate effect of their fuck. 'It was a mistake,' he said.

Still Julien stared, the stare demanding more.

'A very big mistake,' Max said. And then, 'We got too close.'

'How close?'

He spread his hand. 'You know.'

'Fuck, Max. What have you told them?'

'Told who?'

'Your wife. Anyone. The police.'

'I told them nothing.'

'Louise?'

'No. Nothing. I said there was nothing to tell.'

'I see.' Julien poured himself tea. 'Why are you telling me this?'

'Not sure, Jay. To clear the head.' He stretched back and reached arms towards the overhead beams. 'Confession time.'

'You're not the confessing type, Max.'

'Not usually. I don't usually have much to confess.'

He pulled up his trouser leg a few inches and pushed down the sock. There was the neat blue-black image of the owl. 'I got a tattoo, too.'

'A tattoo, too,' Julien mimicked. He looked closer. 'To whit to woo, a tattoo too. What got into you?'

'Midsummer madness. I don't know really. First I sort of fell in love with Sylvie Renard—'

'You mean?'

'I mean Sylvie Renard.'

'You fell in love with Sylvie Renard and fucked Helen White?' Julien was laughing.

'Seems so.'

'And got a tattoo-too as well.'

'As well and in addition—yes.'

They had ordered tagines, Max's chicken, Julien's lamb, both with aubergines, prunes and couscous, and the plates were arriving at their table. For a time they were quiet, eating and murmuring appreciatively.

'Why on earth would you . . .' Julien began.

'I agree,' Max said. 'It was idiotic, but so is the question.'

'What question?'

'Yours. Why would I?'

Julien shrugged. 'You mean because there's no answer.'

'No answer. It happened, that's all.'

'Have you thought about consequences? She's a student, isn't she?'

'Not one of mine. Not in one of my courses—but yes, a student. Enrolled. If she laid a complaint I'd be in trouble. But she won't.'

'You sure?'

'Yes I'm sure. I know one can be wrong about such things, but I'm sure.'

'Because?'

'Because I feel I know her, and we like one another. Don't grin, Julien—it's important. She's obsessed with a poem I wrote years ago. I think she thinks she's rescuing the buried poet in me. She doesn't want to harm me.'

'Isn't she the one you told me was . . .' He waved a hand in vague circles. 'Mad, so to speak?'

'So to speak, yes. Bipolar—or that's what she says. On lithium. It seems to be under control.'

'You'd better hope she stays on it.'

'Listen, Jay, there's something about her that's fundamentally . . . *benign*. I trust her. I trust her goodness.' He hesitated and then rushed on. 'I trust her purity of intent.'

If Julien felt inclined to laugh at this he suppressed it. He nodded and his expression seemed to say he was interested, he was listening. 'But if she stole the picture,' he said.

'Well, yes, that's hard to deal with.'

'Do you have a plan?'

'I need to find her, and if she did take it I need to get it back, smartly—in secret. In the meantime Louise has told the police she's sure her relatives have it. And maybe they have. At least that's keeping everyone's eyes off me.'

Julien was looking down at his plate. 'My tagine has apricots.'

'Mine too,' Max said. 'They're good, aren't they?'

8.

LE MONDE

LOUISE READ ONE MORE TIME the report that had come from the editorial committee on the text she had submitted, her edition of *L'Éducation Sentimentale* with introduction and notes. It was some time since she had received it but she still returned to it for reassurance. It was all affirmative—'sets a new standard of editing and annotation . . .', 'scholars and students will be in her debt . . .', 'clarity and concision . . .', 'every reader of Flaubert . . .', 'a hallmark for the future . . .', 'confirms her pre-eminence among . . .'

She had felt faint with relief when it came. Max had said as much; so had other colleagues who had helped her and would be acknowledged and thanked in a foreword. But this was the document that made it official; put it beyond doubt. Her authority was established. Even she could believe in it.

In the letter that came with the report there were details about book production, a launch planned for mid-year, 2015. That was when Max's conference (or *journée d'études*—she didn't think a decision on what it was to be called had yet been made) on World War I poets was to happen. She would make sure there was no overlap.

And then she wondered whether that was an old habit she needed to break. Why should her launch and his conference not happen at the same time; even on the same day? Or her book launch and his—the big editing job that would attract so much attention because it was a French classic, and his, the little Lessing-Naipaul book he was suddenly so sure about, and which would not attract much notice here in Paris? Or should they happen on either side of the Channel, hers here, his in London? How much were they, he and she, still a unit, and for how much longer? She noticed that she asked herself this question, not sure of an answer, but without the panic that would once have accompanied it.

Last night she had dreamed of Frank Beauchamp, with whom, young and naïve, she had been briefly in love. In the dream she was with him in the villa on the Golfo Paradiso. The pines beyond the windows were very green and the sea very blue. Jean-Claude and Julie were there, but not Max. Frank was reading them a story, and kept looking up from the book and winking. She found this upsetting because it seemed to align her with him against the children, and she was not able to tell him to stop. And then they were leaving in a very big car, driven by Max now—Frank was gone—and she noticed there was a cat on the back seat with the children. Max pointed out that there was a cat door so the animal could come and go. She struggled for words in English to express her astonishment, and could only think of, 'Shit, Max, that's *amazing!*' which seemed very funny, and woke her up.

Once awake, she had wakened herself further by trying to interpret the dream, which she thought was why she was able to remember it now. It was as though the almost forgotten Frank Beauchamp had really been Max. And yet the dream person had not been quite Max—not the real Max, the father of her children. That was why the dream had substituted Frank. He was a caricature Max, not the man she had banished downstairs, or who had banished himself there, and who had written that concise and elegant page she'd read the morning she called in at his apartment. That was the morning he had more or less admitted to being in love with someone—she assumed it must be with the young English woman Helen ('of Troy' had been his joke) who had written him a letter and signed off with '*Je t'embrasse*', and who had somehow persuaded him to visit the grave of her fraudulent guru, Gurdjieff.

Someone famous had said 'in dreams begin responsibilities'. It was a striking aphorism, but it wasn't true. Dreams—hers anyway—were like parodies of reality. Leave dreams to the Freudians and Jungians, she thought. It was better to get on and deal with the realities than waste time with the parody.

But then she couldn't quite resist asking herself what the cat door in the dream had *meant*. It was a way of escape—for the cat. So what was the cat? Did it have to represent something? A Jungian archetype? A Freudian child? The book Max would write, or her own just completed work on Flaubert?

Maybe the cat was just a cat—the one that in English 'sat on the mat'.

And now that she was really awake she remembered the forgotten thing that had been sitting all this while on her shoulder: 'the picture' was gone, stolen. She wept, at first with grief at the loss, and then with anger, the tears becoming bitter at the thought that her relatives, who had failed to defeat her by legal means, had resorted to crime.

Would she ever see it again? She didn't think so.

IT WAS 8 OCTOBER 2014, a Thursday, and because Jacques Derrida, that great Libran and her tormentor, had been on this day dead exactly ten years, Helen White, thinking it an anniversary worthy of commemoration, and visiting her boyfriend Hugh Pennington in Oxford, decided they should see a French movie, just (she said) as a 'recognition', a bow of the head, a dip of the lid, in Derrida's direction; and by chance there was one, a suitable one, said to be full of lovely ambiguities, and made by the writer Michel Houellebecq about himself, or a character called Houellebecq, a writer kidnapped by three amateurs who forced him into a metal box and took him away from Paris into the French countryside, believing naïvely that, because he was French and internationally famous, the president of the republic would pay a generous ransom for his release. The movie was a comedy, in which the Stockholm syndrome worked in reverse, kidnappers converted to the opinions of, and taking sides with, the kidnapped rather than the other way about. Houellebecq, dead-pan and comic, played the title role of Houellebecq, and the script was one Helen was sure Derrida would have applauded, and around which he would have danced a rich texture of cynicism and mystery, obfuscation and ferocity. This movie was showing at the Phoenix in Walton Street, and they had, first, a French dinner and wine at the Café Blanc in the same street, in the suburb with the lovely name of Jericho, all in easy walking distance of the canal, where was moored the houseboat Hugh was occupying at a reduced rent on the understanding that he was its caretaker, and its guard against thieves and vandals.

The day before, the Wednesday, browsing at the Albion Beatnik Bookstore in the same quarter, Helen had found a novel, *Offshore* by Penelope Fitzgerald, which had won the Booker Prize in 1979. Based (so an accompanying information sheet explained) on Fitzgerald's own life, it was about a group of people living in a houseboat on the Thames; and because of its subject Helen decided she and Hugh would begin reading it together, and would continue their conversation about it by email and Skype when she returned to Paris. Scientist Hugh, in order, he said, to make himself a suitable person to be teamed up in bed and at breakfast with Helen, and a suitable father for any children they might have along the way, had joined the Albion Beatnik reading group, and would make *Offshore* his suggestion for a title in the coming months. But, because the copy Helen had found was a first edition, it was beyond her idea of a reasonable price, and she might well have stolen it, thinking 'for Hugh' as she did so, but he, watching over her shoulder, had stopped her from sliding it into her carry-all. So they had walked on, all the way into town (stopping for tea and cakes at the Mitre in the High), and sure enough had found a paperback edition at Blackwell's and bought the two remaining copies, one each. It was not, Helen knew, an entirely propitious choice, at least in the sense that the houseboat in the novel founders and sinks; but likely to be amusing and upbeat in the telling.

'Hugh's Houseboat', she called his dwelling; he was 'Houseboat Hugh'; and together he and she were 'Helen-and-Hugh-in-a-Houseboat', which was lexically nicer than Helen and Max in any boat at all—though she could not pretend to herself that she would not have loved it had the improbable latter been the case. The deck of the houseboat had canvas chairs for sitting in the sun, and ropes and poles for negotiating the locks and tying up to docks, and many potted plants, some of them flowering shrubs, others herbs for the kitchen. It was a cross between a sailor's yard and a garden, and she had named it 'the Guard's Garden Yard', shortened to the G.G.Y.; and it was right there, in the G.G.Y., that Hugh, playing in the night 'Greensleeves' and related Tudor melodies on his violin after they had seen *The Kidnapping of Michel Houellebecq*, asked Helen, seriously and solemnly, to come and set up house—set up houseboat—with him here in Jericho; and, under a moonlit Oxford sky pricked by dreaming spires, she promised that she would, though there was one small matter (she called it a course of lectures though that was not entirely truthful) in Paris to be completed first.

'So we're engaged,' she told herself, and tried it out in her head. Engaged. Engaged. That was the word on the toilet door when there was someone in there doing something urgent, something necessary—or disreputable. But she would not try that joke out on Hugh—it might upset him.

'That makes me your fiancée,' she said.

'It does,' he said, and seemed pleased.

●

SYLVIE PLAYED FOR MAX IN one of the practice rooms at the École Normale Supérieure, where a helpful concierge accepted small gifts and allowed her in when there was a practice room free. Sylvie led Max through the main entrance and downstairs to a basement, where she spoke briefly to her friend in his lodge.

Coming out again she told Max, 'I've said you're my page turner. Do you read music?'

'Eat good bread, dear father. I read anything.'

'Not that anyone is likely to check.'

'It will be an excuse.'

'An excuse?'

'To stand close.'

Along the downstairs corridors there were notice-boards announcing rooms to let, instruments for sale, offers of private tuition, appeals for baby-sitters. In practice room five the floors were wooden, the walls painted a pale (or faded) halfway between green and beige. Old posters of concerts and recitals sagged or hung sideways on the walls above oil radiators. 'It's rather drab,' Sylvie said, looking around.

'I'm here to hear.'

'Here to hear,' she repeated. 'Just as well.'

There were two Yamaha uprights. Sylvie played the A note two or three times and a chord on one, then on the other. 'You choose,' she said, and he chose the second.

She took out the music she'd brought. 'Nothing from memory,' she said. She sat a while, pulled the seat closer, sat again, exercising her fingers, interlocking them, while Max stood to her left, waiting.

She played first a Scriabin fantasy, and then a Bach suite. 'The English Suite—for you, Max,' she said.

A Prokofiev sonata came next.

Occasionally she stopped, murmured a word as much to herself as to him, and began again a few bars back; but mostly the works were played straight through, fluently. He watched the fingers and marvelled.

He did not say much. What was there to say? He stood very still, hearing every note, feeling them sometimes in his scalp and down his spine, and thinking how mysterious it was that interpreters of a work of art could seem to assume into themselves its quality, refinement, power, even its greatness. He had seen actors grow in stature as they took on major roles. Sometimes it was best, if you wanted the illusion to last, not to hear them interviewed afterwards.

Sylvie now had for him a new authority, and yet nothing had

changed. She was still the young woman who had said she was going to buy shoes as a response to 'climate change and all the rest of it'.

Some dim and yet conscious part of his brain had this conversation with itself; the rest was transfixed, enchanted, transported—because it wanted to be, and because the performance was up to the task, equal to it. He had not departed from reality; or, if he had, it was with a return ticket in his back pocket. Goodbye, Reality—I'll be back!

So he saw Sylvie, whose playing could be as sensitive one moment, and as powerful another, as the music required, growing. If it were all an illusion, the illusion was confirmed—and what is a confirmed illusion if it is not for the moment a fact? Some part of his mind knew all this.

He supposed that, between items, she must have seen the effect her performance was having—that his eyes shone one moment and looked stunned the next. He didn't try to hide his feelings. Maybe he was even acting them out for her.

It was past four o'clock when her hour at the keyboard was over. They walked to a café in the rue des Écoles and had coffee and cake. At Le Champo, the little cinema next door, which specialised in revivals, *Les Vacances de Monsieur Hulot* was showing. On a whim they joined the queue, students and the elderly mostly, and watched Jacques Tati's long-legged slapstick—his butterfly net, fishing rod and picnic basket; his eccentric tennis serve with a small, polite bow when he served an ace; the pipe the hotelier had to remove from his mouth so he could understand the name, *Hu-lot*, given at the desk.

Then they walked again, towards the Panthéon. When they found themselves outside the church Max had last visited for Uncle Henri's funeral, Sylvie said they must go in. She would light a candle for them. It might protect them, or bring them good fortune.

Indoors, her knees-bend towards the distant altar and the elevated Jesus impressed him as something you had to have learned as a child to do so naturally, effortlessly, perhaps even requiring, or at least enhanced by, a significant degree of faith. He thought of his two children, and hoped not.

He plundered a small eel-skin coin-purse Louise had brought him from Liguria to pay for Sylvie's candle. The coins clanged into the tin box, letting any sharp-eared priest or functionary know that the prayer, or whatever the observance was to be, had been paid for—overpaid, which might increase the attention the Powers were able to give to it. The candle, one of the more expensive ones, was blood red, and she lit it and placed it at the chapel to the Virgin where her prayer was said with what might have been (going on appearances) sincerity and devotion. Max liked the scene, so rich in symbolism—the handsome young woman on her knees before the sad effigy, and the ruby-red candle.

As they made their way out and down the steps to the street he asked, 'Is it wise to draw her attention to us?'

'Our Lady is very forgiving,' she said; and because she didn't laugh, or even smile, he had no idea what he was supposed to make of this. The bright eyes in a straight face suggested irony, but how could he be sure? When he knew her better he would know how to read her. And then he wondered, would he ever know her better, and whether that was what he wanted.

A café-restaurant, Le Petit Prince, was not far from the church, and they found themselves a table there. Sylvie explained to the waiter that she was vegetarian (something else Max had not known), and chose accordingly. 'And you, Monsieur?'

Max ordered duck à l'orange. They both chose *tarte fine aux pommes* to follow, which had to be ordered now, in advance, because it was fresh-baked, not precooked and reheated.

The restaurant was a narrow room with a bar at the entrance, and a stairway halfway down the room which went up and stopped at the ceiling, now wallboarded over where the gap to the floor above had been. Pot plants, ornaments and candlesticks decorated the stairs, and among these a small dog, very cute, his head between the rails, looked out fondly at the customers. Max got up and patted him and his hand was generously licked. 'I think he must be the little prince,' Max said.

He asked had she read the paper on Edward Thomas that Helen White had offered for their conference.

'I've had a quick glance,' Sylvie said. 'There's not a lot about the war.'

'Because Thomas didn't write about it.'

When she looked at him with an 'I rest my case' expression, Max said, 'He died in it. It killed him. He was a poet. Isn't that enough?'

Her expression was still sceptical.

Max said, 'Rupert Brooke was killed by a mosquito bite.'

'But he wrote about the war.'

'Before he'd seen it. He wrote about a fantasy of glory. Each case is different.'

'So—you liked it,' she said. 'You thought it was good.'

'I thought it was interesting. Worth considering. Helen's an interesting young woman.'

Sylvie nodded. 'Helen,' she said. 'First names.'

'Helen and Max,' he said. 'Max and Helen.'

'Very good,' Sylvie said. 'Excellent.' Her smile had an edge. 'Staff and students getting on well together. What could be better?'

'She's not an undergraduate, Sylvie.'

'Oxford graduate. Yes I know.'

She was beginning to be bored, he could see that, or pretending to be, and he said, 'You can yawn if you like, I won't be offended.'

She mimicked a yawn. 'That's for your Helen White.'

He changed direction and told her that her playing of Scriabin had been brilliant.

'Thank you, Max. It wasn't brilliant, and I'm sure you know that, but it was sufficient for the brilliance of Scriabin . . .'

'To be heard,' he said. 'Yes it was. I heard it. I loved it. Thank you.'

But a cloud had gone over their sun. Scriabin was somewhere behind them, along with Monsieur Hulot's fishing net and tennis racket. Sylvie's eyes seemed to search Max for clues, revelations. He was glad to be here, sitting with her in Le Petit Prince; and he was not sorry to be where they were in this conversation, somehow at odds, mysteriously. It meant that Helen White was there with them, an invisible third party.

Sylvie fiddled with her knife and fork, and then looked up at him again. 'I read somewhere recently that the latest information from astronomers—possibly from the Hubble telescope, I'm not sure—is that there are more galaxies in the universe than was thought. Many more. Two trillion.'

He said, 'I've never been sure what a trillion is.'

'Does it matter?'

'No of course not. It's a lot.'

'An unimaginable lot.'

'How big is a galaxy?'

'I think ours is the Milky Way.'

'Jesus!'

'Two trillion of those,' she said. 'Inconceivable.'

He felt himself frowning. Where was she taking him?

She said, 'When I was a child I had trouble with infinity. I couldn't imagine the sky—the heavens—going on forever, so

I would put a sort of vast glass wall right around the outside of everything. That was the extent of the universe—I mean of space. And then the thought would creep up on me—what's on the other side of the glass? It was impossible to conceive of an outside limit. But it was equally impossible to imagine space going on forever. To me that still makes sense.'

'Yes it does. Horribly, it makes sense.'

'Horrible, yes it is.' Her eyes were keen. 'Two trillion galaxies—and that's only as far as modern instruments have been able to measure. So why not give up the idea of limit and accept that infinity is infinite? There's nothing out there but more of the same. More and more and more, on and on. It's like a really distressing, really black, really incomprehensible joke.'

He was thinking space, yes, but time had to come into it. But what he said was, 'And yet you pray.'

'I don't pray. I play. I go through the motions. I pretend there are limits, and a God up there keeping an eye on me.'

He nodded. 'I understand that, of course.' And then, 'But you don't believe it.'

'How could anyone? Do you?'

'No.'

The recommended *tarte fine aux pommes*, by the time they got to it, was very good but it passed almost unremarked. They ate it in silence until, remembering 'the picture', he said, 'So now let me tell you something about Helen White—something that won't cause you to yawn.'

•

VERY LATE THAT NIGHT, OR early next morning, when they had made love in the downstairs apartment and had slept for some hours, Sylvie woke and said, 'Are you awake?'

'Yes,' Max said. And then, struggling, 'No, but I can be.'

'I just woke up feeling envious of your wife.'

'Mmm.' He tried and failed to stay conscious.

'Are you asleep, Max?'

'No.'

'What did I say?'

'You're . . . That you're jealous of Louise.'

'No. Wrong. I said I was envious.'

'Envious, right.'

'Because she has her professional life. Such a good and successful one. And she has a husband and two children.'

He shook himself out of sleep. 'You can have all that, Sylv.'

'You think?'

'Of course.' And then, not thinking, or perhaps thinking too clearly, 'You need to find someone nearer your own age.'

After a silence long enough for him to slip back into sleep she said, 'Max.'

'What?'

'Could you please not call me "Sylv".'

'Oh sure, of course, sorry.' And once more sleep had hold of him.

Later he woke. She was sound asleep now, hanging on to his upper arm, hugging it to her, with his hand, passive, clamped between her knees. It was as if the whole limb were something separate—a big doll, a detachable piece of him to be loved and possessed. There were some lines of William Blake that had come into his dream:

Never seek to tell thy love
Love that never told should be

but he could not remember how they went on.

•

NEXT MORNING, MONSIEUR FERNEY SAW them standing out in the courtyard, holding hands, waiting while Skipper did his business. Max had the polythene bag for it ready in his left hand, and the young lady had a piece of toast she was eating in her right.

Later, as she was leaving, she and Monsieur Ferney confronted one another by chance. It was not so much a confrontation as an encounter, entirely pleasant, in which they wished one another good day and smiled. He did not think she was the kind of woman you paid for sex. Too entirely respectable, nicely dressed and groomed, with expensive shoes and a casual yet cared-for coiffure. He thought he could smell verbena as she passed. Probably one of Monsieur Max's younger colleagues at the Sorbonne. Different from the one he'd seen him with a day or so before the picture disappeared. That one had had a strange look about her—he'd found it hard to describe to the police officer when he came back. 'Wild and woolly,' Monsieur Ferney had said. 'Sort of, you know, *scattered*.'

He was pleased about this young woman. Monsieur needed a friend and some loving comfort now that Madame had turfed him out from upstairs and didn't even take him with her on holiday.

•

HELEN AND MAX CAME AROUND corners from opposite directions and stopped. She felt herself blushing. 'Max!'

'Helen! You're back.'

'Yes, and I have new digs.'

'That's good, is it?'

'Nearer . . .' She meant to the Sorbonne Nouvelle. 'In the rue Cardinal Lemoine.' But he wasn't listening. She said, 'Did you get my paper?' He was going to ask her something. 'World War One,' she said, prompting him. 'Edward Thomas.'

'Yes of course. Didn't I tell you? I thought I'd emailed. I meant to. It's good. Interesting.'

'So I can . . .'

'There's only the question of whether there's enough about the war. In his poems, I mean.'

'Well he didn't . . . He was killed. It killed him.'

'Sylvie was anxious about that.'

'Sylvie?'

'Renard. Listen, Helen, the day we spent together . . .'

She blushed again, and stopped herself from saying it was the best day of her life. That would have been ridiculous—the kind of exaggeration she was trying to teach herself not to go in for.

'You came upstairs with me,' he said. 'The picture . . .' He was staring at her so intently. 'It's gone. It was taken.'

'What picture?' Something had made her go very calm, very cool.

'The picture. The Cézanne, for fuck's sake . . .' He looked left and right, pulled her to one side of the corridor, and went on, controlling his voice. 'You and I were up there, we looked at it, we talked about it, and next day it was gone.'

'That's a surprise.'

'It's . . .' He stopped. And then, angrily, 'What do you mean, it's a surprise? Of course it's a fucking surprise.'

She said nothing. She could see he found it hard to say what came next, but he rose to it: 'Did you take it?'

'No.'

'Are you sure?'

'Yes.'

He looked into her eyes. 'Helen, this is serious. It's not a game.

It's a valuable . . . It's—'

'A Cézanne. I know.'

'The police have been called.'

'That's good I should think.'

He seemed not to know where to go next. She said, 'I've been listening to you lecture this week.'

'What?' He was disconcerted. 'What are you talking about?'

'I sat in on two of your lectures. They were awfully good.'

He frowned. 'When was that?'

'Last Thursday, and yesterday.'

She could see he was thinking that this could not be true; that if she had been in one of his classes he would have seen her. 'It was in the Grand Amphithéâtre,' she said. 'There's a little stairway to the upper seats at the back. I sat on the stairs. You can hear every word there without being seen. I thought it was brilliant, especially yesterday.'

He said, 'The picture, Helen. The Cézanne.'

'Yes, I know. I loved it.'

'And you stole it.'

'No.'

'Are you sure?'

'Fairly sure.' She meant it as a joke.

'Fairly sure you . . .' Even at this moment, he could not quite suppress a grin, as if they were sharing it. 'Could we just focus for a moment?'

'If you like, Max.'

'What I'd like, Helen, is for you to understand that this is something really and truly serious—something not funny at all, and something that lithium won't correct, OK? If you have that painting you should tell me and together we'll find a way of returning it without anyone knowing.'

She bridled at the mention of her medication. Coolly she said, 'I'll check through my things.'

He grabbed her by the upper arms, as if to shake her, then let her go at once, and again looked around, nervous that this lapse might have been seen, or picked up on the corridor's CCTV. 'I'm sorry.' He breathed deeply. 'We're friends, aren't we?'

'Yes, Max.' She meant it, and said it as if she did. 'We're friends.'

'So you must behave like one.'

'Yes.'

'If you have the picture, you must let your friend help you. If you have it you're in trouble, you understand?'

She said, 'I suppose if I had it, we'd both be in trouble.'

He half turned away, controlling his first impulse, and then turned back to face her again. 'Well that might be true. So we need to help one another.'

'Yes.'

'Do you have it?'

'No.'

'Did you take it?'

'I don't think so.'

The impatience returned and was suppressed. He stared at her. 'Please, Helen.'

She met his gaze. 'I thought your lecture yesterday was one of the most brilliant I've ever listened to.' She meant that too.

He seemed somehow defeated, deflated—and then it was as if he'd decided to forget the missing picture for a moment and enjoy the praise. He said, 'The best lectures are when you've been wrestling with a problem and you still haven't quite worked it out, and then the answer only comes at the last moment, in a rush while you're expounding it in the lecture room. It can only happen once for each problem. When you have the answer it goes into the lecture next time round. It's still a good fish, but no longer fresh.'

They stood a moment, reflecting on good fish and fresh fish, until she said, 'Are you writing new poems?'

'No poems. I'm doing my Lessing-Naipaul book.' As he said this he felt suddenly cheerful. 'It's going to be good.'

It was as if a shot of something like electricity passed between them. 'Gosh!' she said. 'That's so exciting.'

'It's lit crit,' he said, 'but it's *writing* too. People don't think lit crit can be beautiful, but it can.'

She nodded, thinking, I could have this man's child—and then suppressed a laugh at the thought of how that would frighten him if she should say it aloud. She looked into his eyes and noticed how keen and clear they were, especially for a man in his forties. Cleopatra eyes. Age had not withered them nor smoking staled . . .

She felt alarmed at herself, at the strength of her own feelings, and looked at her watch as if she had somewhere to go.

'About the picture,' he said.

'Yes, darling Max,' she said. 'Yes yes yes,' and kissed him firmly on the mouth, three times. 'Must rush.'

And that's what she did—rushed—down the corridor, out into the quadrangle and the street and down into the crowds on the Boulevard Saint-Michel. She did not know how far he pursued her, if at all, but when she stopped for breath at the next intersection and looked around there was no sign of him.

9.

SYLVIE

AND HELEN

AUTUMN ARRIVED ON TIME, AND the two trees in the courtyard Max looked out on turned a quite showman's orange-yellow or yellow-gold, depending on what the light was doing—and it was all, as any photographer would tell you, a collaboration with the light. Still at this date, the first of November, a Saturday, there were, among the leaves, a few pallid green survivors, brave rather than bravura, and soon to die. It was a collaboration too, quite as significantly, with the wind, which came and went, or refused to come, sending down (or not) showers of orange-yellow gold over his small aromatic garden and over the paved courtyard, the protected enclosure that had all the secret charm of Paris as it had appeared to him, and had captured him, in the uncertainty of his youth. There was, erratically, sunshine too, but it was the first sun of autumn rather than the last of summer, with little of summer left in it, hardly a hint, only a memory. It was the sun of the northern-hemisphere November, and the harder it tried to be better the more manifest its failure seemed.

As Max watched from his window, the casual gardener employed by the *syndic* was sweeping leaves from the paved area with a broom. He was armed also with a blower (no modern gardener is without one) with which he would soon blow leaves out of the beds and hedges. Here in the shelter of the courtyard his blower when he used it would be the worst of winds. Out in the boulevards, where the real wind blew, the fall was more advanced, and the leaves, most often plain brown, were showering down and clattering along the gutters and pavements faster than the men in their green sweeping machines could keep ahead of them. The trees in the Jardin des Plantes, and in the Luxembourg Gardens, had lost their summer shapes, and the reflecting pool of the Medici Fountain was so cluttered it reflected nothing but its own failure.

Sitting there in the window embrasure, Max was invaded by a particular memory of his early days in Paris. He had been there perhaps six or eight months of a bad summer, much of which he felt had been spent hunting for street names and managing maps in wind and rain, getting lost, finding his way, congratulating himself for having done well, or cursing himself for failure. This particular day it was autumn, November like today, fine but cold, and already the drunks and homeless ones were lying down over the pavement grilles to warm themselves in the air coming up from the Métro; and, as Max was walking towards the river in the morning sun, he found himself wondering what had changed, what was the different (and wonderful) feel about this day? It was then he recognised that he was walking freely, not checking constantly where he was, because he knew and didn't need even to think about it. Paris, or this part of it, had become his city, and he was its inhabitant. And just then, as he was crossing the Pont de Sully from left to right bank, he looked downriver and there was Notre-Dame in full morning sun, with its twin towers, its iron spire and flying buttresses, looking like the great ship of souls, sailing towards him up the river. It took him by surprise and he was faint with the beauty of it, and of the city, and had to stop and lean on the balustrade and stare. He tried to think of a French poem to suit the moment, knowing there must be many, but could only bring to mind Apollinaire's 'The Mirabeau Bridge', and the one by Baudelaire in which the poet crosses the Carrousel Bridge, and neither of those seemed to match the place and the time. So he quoted to himself T.S. Eliot's lines about the Thames and they seemed to fit well enough because the trees over the Seine were also shedding their leaves:

> The river's tent is broken: the last fingers of leaf
> Clutch and sink into the wet bank. The wind
> Crosses the brown land, unheard. The nymphs are departed.

He was, that day, already in love with Louise Simon, who was resisting him with a sort of French—or perhaps it was just female—ambiguity and cunning. The problem, insofar as she was willing or able to make it clear, was his foreignness, his 'Britishness'. It made no difference to tell her he was not British, he was a New Zealander. And when he tried to explain the differences, their subtleties and declensions, she said he was being needlessly subtle and essentially boring—and he thought so too.

'One day you will want to go back there,' she said. 'Or to Britain.'

'Only if you were with me,' he'd said. It had felt like a

commitment, a promise for the future.

The gardener had gone now, taking his portable wind with him, and Max moved to sit outdoors in the courtyard as if to encourage the sun, as if to tell it not to be faint-hearted or sorry for itself: there was honour in old age. Like a true Frenchman he took *Le Monde* to read out there. Today it was featuring the tortures ISIS militants had inflicted on their Western captives before releasing those for whom the governments of Spain and France had (though denying it) paid a ransom, and beheading one by one, and by hand, the two Americans and two British whose governments had announced that no blood money would be paid.

Max moved on to an inner-page piece about the precarious health of the young in outer Paris compared to those at the centre; and then to one from Marseilles, where an authorised marriage celebrant, a Muslim, had declined to marry a lesbian couple because he had been advised he would burn in hell if he did.

In the section on the arts and culture he read that Patrick Modiano, France's new Nobel laureate, whose award had been announced in October, was 'unknown and unread in his own country'. Was this true? The bookshops now were full of his work, displayed with their red banners announcing the prize. Louise, who had read most of them, thought the award spoke for intelligibility against the old New Wave novelists and their apologists. Enough of Claude Simon, Alain Robbe-Grillet, and Roland Barthes, and long live the clarity, limpidity, transparency for which French literature had always been celebrated! Louise saw it as an indirect vote for Flaubert, whom the New Wave novelists and critics had disparaged.

Max came now to the 'economy and enterprise' pages, where a philosopher, Pierre Zaoui, was drawing subtle distinctions, not only between a *crisis* and a *catastrophe* in the money world, but between two kinds of *catastrophe*—the 1929-jumping-out-of-windows kind in which even wealthy families lost everything, and the less serious kind of 2008 in which life went on for the rich, whose loss was a reduction of their wealth, not an end to it. In support of all this, Machiavelli was quoted (as between 'good luck' and 'well done' the balance was fifty-fifty), and also Nietzsche (great events approach like doves, not with matching clamour). This piece, it seemed to Max, was not so much high finance as highbrow finance; a kind of brain-straining and heartless entertainment; 'Money' for the *Le Mondeans*.

The wind was really blowing now, even here in the shelter of the courtyard, making it difficult to keep the paper together, and Max moved indoors. He should be thinking about the *Habilitation* jury he was to be part of, and the presentation they were to examine. The candidate was Sylvie's English friend whose name for the moment he couldn't remember—Elise perhaps, or Elsie. Yes, it was Elsie. Sylvie had told him about how they'd been friends since childhood, exchanging schools and families for periods so each would learn the other's language and culture. ('And cooking,' Sylvie had said, and he'd laughed obligingly, understanding it was that tired old French joke about English cuisine.) He'd thought perhaps she'd been on the brink of asking him to give her friend a helping hand, or at least to go easy on her, but then had recognised that this would be improper and stopped short of it. Just to tell him they were old friends was enough.

But Elsie Henderson (yes, that was her name)—Elsie's subject, the literature of French colonialism, was not one he had ever studied closely, and his presence on the jury was, he knew, just a case of making up the numbers. There were to be five professors and he was certainly the fifth. All the more reason for looking again at the presentation this Elsie Henderson had put before them; but, standing at the window again, he allowed his mind to drift back to the comfort of that long-ago November when his epiphany on a bridge over the Seine had made him feel for a moment that he had become a Parisian, a true *flâneur*, and that his times of trouble were over.

•

SYLVIE HAD TEACHING THE DAY of Elsie's *Habilitation*, and came and went as her timetable allowed. She was nervous for her friend and hoped the professors would not be too tough on her. The Salle Bourjois had red chairs for the audience and a matching red cloth on the table behind which the jury were sitting. Elsie stood at a black lectern, her papers sorted and ready, facing the jury and with the audience at her back. Beside her was a professor with whom she had worked closely—her *garant*, her advocate in effect. Behind the jury, elevated on a pillar and frowning down at Elsie as she spoke, was the marble head of another grand personage from the Sorbonne's past. On the wall at her back, facing down the room, a very large tapestry represented a hunting scene. The wall to her left was all windows, tall and broad and divided into squares.

Elsie's friends and relations had been invited, and Sylvie recognised both her parents and one sister among the crowd. Students and staff of the university who had an interest in her subject could attend, and there were some already assembled. So, technically, could any passer-by looking for entertainment, or simply wanting to come in out of the cold; but the Sorbonne's security was tight these days, and Sylvie could see none of the rough sleepers and vagrants who might otherwise have been among Elsie's audience. The examination process would continue through the morning, or as long as necessary.

If Elsie was nervous it didn't show. Her voice was steady and her hands didn't shake. She began by formally thanking the university, the jury, her advocate, the audience . . . There seemed no end to these gratitudes, which Sylvie recognised as part of the process. But soon her friend was putting her case. As Elsie began to speak about the novels of Camus and Marguerite Duras, Sylvie watched Max's face. He looked very distinguished up there, in his robes and among the professoriate—but was he listening? Yes, he was. He was interested, she could see that. That was good—his interest was engaged. The light was shining on his head and she could see a small patch of silver-grey. That would suit him, she thought, as it had suited Bill Clinton to let his hair go white rather than dying it as Reagan had done. Max's eyes were lowered towards the desk in front, but now he looked up and around the room and, after a moment, saw her looking at him from the side aisle. He raised his eyebrows just a little, the faintest signal to her, and there was a matching half smile.

My God he's lovely, she thought. What a pity.

•

HELEN TOOK THE MÉTRO FROM Cardinal Lemoine to Sèvres-Babylone, changed and took the line north towards Porte de la Chapelle, changed at Saint-Lazare, and went two stops to the Place de Clichy. She had been reading a novel by Georges Perec about a young man, a student in Paris, who decides to drop out of everything—the university, examinations, friends, ambition, work, play—in effect to go to sleep, to stop living. It fascinated her because it was the reverse of what Gurdjieff advocated—that you must work hard, making a continuous effort to be awake, to be aware of every passing moment, and thus to create a soul. It was the story of willed depression—the deliberate welcoming of what sometimes enveloped her even while she tried to fight it off. It was an account, a fiction, of a young man working, not to create a soul, but to be rid of one.

In the end he fails to achieve what he's aiming for—the ultimate indifference. His project has been a kind of egotism, a wish to be special, especially blighted, cursed, cast out, reviled. He is none of these things, and he tells himself, at last, to stop talking to himself like a man in a dream. 'You are not the nameless master of the world, the one on whom history has lost its grip, the one who no longer feels the rain falling.'

The book ends with this awakening, which comes to him on a rainy day in the Place de Clichy, and that was why Helen, with what she recognised was a dogged literalness, was going there today, when the rain was falling.

She stood on a corner in the rain, enjoying the sound of its myriad small feet on her umbrella, its coldness when it found its way on to her right arm, and the feeling that now and then it was putting fine jewels in her hair, while she tried to think herself into the state of mind of Perec's student, coming back into the world after a long self-imposed absence; waking to the discomforts and pleasures of existence, as if for a long moment they had gone away.

And what came to her first, sharp and clear, at this moment at the busy intersection of Avenue de Clichy and Boulevard des Batignolles, was the recognition that she might be pregnant, and that she did not know for sure whether, if she was, it would be Max's child or Hugh's. She'd made love to Hugh in Oxford, with no precautions apart from an idea of the safe time of the month. The first time with Max she thought there had been a condom, but not the second.

The possibility of pregnancy did not distress her, but she was bothered by the question, which of them, Max or Hugh, should she tell: either or neither—or both? Which would she prefer? And when should she break the news? Better wait; better be sure. She'd had these scares before.

And now the rain fell less like a fine mist, more heavy and persistent, the cars splashed through puddles, the air grew colder, and she went back down into the Métro, to its warm, dry air, and the smell of rubber on metal that always reminded her of the excitement of being in Paris for the first time.

•

SYLVIE AND MAX MET IN the evening after the *Habilitation*. Sylvie's friend was already gone, her success confirmed by the jury after due deliberation. It had been a solemn moment, the audience called back in, the jury, the candidate, her advocate, the audience all on their feet in silence, and then the affirmative result read out by the senior professor, followed by excitement, applause and congratulation. Drinks had followed and Elsie had finally been taken away for dinner with her family who had come by Eurostar to be witnesses to their daughter's academic triumph.

Sylvie and Max left together and walked first down the boulevard towards the river. She had been gripped by his story about Helen White and the missing Cézanne. But she thought there were gaps in what he'd told her. Why the matching tattoos, for example— what did that mean? And why hadn't he told his wife, and the police, that Helen had been there, in the upstairs apartment, a day or so before the fact that the picture was missing had been noticed?

He said he was afraid for Helen, for the precariousness of her mind. 'She's back in Paris,' he said. 'I ran into her in a corridor. I asked her about the painting. She said she didn't take it.'

'Of course. Did you believe her?'

'Yes and no.'

'Yes? Or no?'

'It's hard to decide. Her behaviour's so unusual. It's as though everything is on the brink of comedy. I can't be quite sure when she's serious.'

'You should tell someone.'

'I don't want to get her into trouble.'

'If she took the picture she's in trouble now—she got herself there.'

'I took her to the apartment. I'm in it with her.'

'Are you?' They walked on in silence a few steps. 'Why are you?'

Max didn't answer. After a while he said, 'I told her if she took the picture she should tell me and we'd think up a way to return it without getting her deeper in.'

'And?'

'And nothing. She just said "Yes yes yes", kissed me three times and rushed off into the street.'

'That's interesting, Max.'

'It wasn't an answer.'

'I mean the kisses. Are you lovers?'

'Of course not.'

They were not going anywhere, just walking and talking—easily, without embarrassment, as if they had known one another in an earlier life. There had been rain in the morning but now the sky had cleared. The winds of earlier in the month had died away, the air was fresh but still. By a roundabout route they reached the Luxembourg Gardens. They were still there on a sort of park bench, talking about Elsie Henderson's *Habilitation* ideas, when the wardens began blowing their whistles announcing sundown and that the gates would soon be locked. The subject of Helen

White had somehow been left behind. Sylvie was sure there was something Max preferred not to tell her but she didn't press him. It was something she had learned with Bertholdt—or rather had learned too late with Bertholdt, and with Max she was not going to repeat the mistake. She would let him keep his secrets.

When they stood up and faced one another he put a flat hand up to the top of her head, showing how tall she was in her heels.

'If I kissed you,' he said, 'I wouldn't have to bend.'

'Try it,' she said, and he did, quite a gentle kiss. The lips were lovely, and he kissed them again.

'We fit one another,' she said.

'We do.' He moved closer against her. 'At every point. But we knew that.'

She said, 'At the *Habilitation* today—I thought you sent me a little signal.'

'I did.'

'You looked very handsome up there with all the grandees.'

'A sham.'

'Not at all. You were where you belong. I thought you looked such a nice guy. And I thought what a pity.'

'What was a pity?'

'Such a nice guy and he will never leave his wife.'

He was silent a moment. 'She might leave me,' he said.

Sylvie patted his shoulder and they moved apart, and on towards the gates. 'What a gamble that would be,' she said.

'You mean for Louise?'

No, that was not what she meant, but she didn't explain.

They were quiet now, calm, good friends, as if (but was it really so?) neither wanted anything of the other. At the lights they crossed the rue de Vaugirard.

'We're not far from my door,' she said. 'You can take me there.'

'And beyond?'

'Beyond?'

'Indoors. Upstairs.'

'Not unless you want to meet Bertholdt again.'

'No, I don't think so. Does he know about our night together?'

'I didn't think he was ready for that. Or that I was.'

'Least said . . .'

'Yes, if we want it mended.'

'Do you?'

'Yes but not yet—and not for ever—you know. Remembering your advice.'

'What was that?'

'My needing a man closer to my own age.'

'That was just midnight ramblings.'

'It was the owl of Minerva. Has Louise seen your tattoo?'

'Not yet,' he said. And then, 'How did you explain your absence that night?'

'Lied, of course. Told him I was coaching Elsie for the *Habilitation*.'

A few steps on she asked, 'Are you going to tell someone about Helen?' When he didn't answer she said, 'You should, you know. If she has it, it's urgent. If not, then no harm's done.'

He said, 'I need to find her again. She's moved—she said to the rue Cardinal Lemoine. I have to give her another chance . . .'

He put an arm around Sylvie's waist, pulled her towards him and kissed her. It was a nice kiss but fraternal. It was as if something had been agreed though it had not quite been spelled out. They were not going to be lovers—not any more.

'*À bientôt*,' he said, and watched as she crossed the street again.

•

BERTHOLDT, ON WATCH IN THE dark at a window, saw Max and Sylvie, arm in arm under the street-lights, coming down the rue de Vaugirard past the railings of the Luxembourg Gardens. Outside the gates, which were already locked, they stopped and talked. Max kissed her, once, and then a second time. That's comprehensive, Bertholdt thought, wincing slightly. They were holding on to one another now. Was that a goodbye-for-ever kind of hug, or just a not-wanting-to-let-go?

He watched as Sylvie crossed the street. On the opposite pavement she turned back and waved. Max returned the wave, waited while she disappeared out of Bertholdt's line of sight, then waved again. When he turned away Bertholdt assumed she was already indoors. A moment later he heard the clank and whine of the lift going down to her.

He took hold of himself. He had felt some anger, but to give way to it would have been absurd. This should be, and was, a welcome confirmation. He would pretend he had seen nothing. He would say nothing.

His rehearsals for *The Ghost Sonata* at last seemed to be working. Everyone agreed he'd made sense of that strangely recalcitrant play. He had done the impossible. 'A miracle,' they were saying.

It was not a miracle—he knew that; just a professional job. But the praise was welcome, and so was the bonus.

If this goes on, he told himself, thinking of Sylvie again, I could be home in Berlin for Christmas with Gertrude and the boys. No strings. No real grounds for weeping or anger on either side—just, 'Thanks for a very nice time. Let's stay friends—maybe even do it again one day. And so goodbye.'

Cool and clean, though not without regrets.

When Sylvie came in he was sitting in his usual chair with a glass of wine and the lights still off so she did not see him there.

She went to the window and looked down, and stood a while.

'So how did it go?' he said.

She jumped. 'Jesus Christ, Bertie!'

She peered around the room and found him in the shadows. 'Why are you sitting in the dark?'

'I'm having a quiet moment.'

She took a deep breath, recovering, calming herself. He supposed she was worrying that he might have been watching from the window. He said again, 'So how did it go?'

'How did it go? What the fuck does that mean?' She was flustered. 'How did what go?'

'I thought today was your friend's—'

'Oh Elsie, of course, the *Habilitation*. Yes, sorry, I was . . .' She took a deep breath. 'Sorry. It went well. She passed—flying colours. I was worried Max—I thought he might give her a hard time, but he didn't. Hardly asked her any questions, and they were patsies, more or less telling her she'd passed before there was even a verdict. I wondered whether he'd read the stuff she'd got ready for them. Max is in a bit of a state . . .'

She was speaking too fast, rattled. He wasn't going to let her know what he knew, but for the moment he wouldn't let her know, either, that she was safe. He was enjoying watching her sweat a little. She had not made these past few weeks easy for him.

'His wife—Max's wife, she has a valuable painting. Well, it's his too, I guess, but it's been in her family for ever, a Cézanne, or supposed to be a Cézanne, not authenticated but they're all sure it is, and suddenly it isn't there.'

'Why don't you sit down?' he said.

She lapsed into the nearest comfortable chair, facing him. It was the reluctant, almost despairing slide of someone expecting at any moment to be hearing accusations and unwelcome truths.

'Do we have to have the lights off?' she said.

'Let me get you a drink.' He said it as if preparing her for the worse that was not to come.

He poured her some of the wine he was drinking, handed it to her with a slight theatrical flourish, and returned to his chair. 'I like this room with just the light coming in from the street,' he said. 'It's soothing. One feels one can be oneself.'

'Good for one,' she said. 'I don't feel that at all.'

She sipped; they both sipped.

'So it's missing,' he said. She didn't respond, and he went on, 'A painting. A Cézanne . . .'

'Said to be.'

'And now it's gone, and your professor—'

'He's not my professor, Bertholdt.'

'No, well, I'm sure he's everyone's professor. I mean Professor Max, the one who told me he was reading about the Holocaust—'

'He told you he was reading Martin Amis.'

'That's the one.'

'Yes, the painting's gone.'

'Stolen?'

'His wife thinks her family have it.'

'So why is he worried?'

'I don't know—that he's worried—'

'You said he was in a state.'

'Did I? Yes I did.' She thought a moment and then seemed to decide that if he wanted this to take time, wanted to spin it out and torment her, she would accept that. 'Max is worried,' she said, 'because he took a student up to their upstairs apartment . . .'

'The one the professor-wife occupies.'

'Yes, but the professor-wife was away on holiday, and after he and the student had been there the picture was gone.'

'So the student stole it.'

'He doesn't know but he thinks she might have. He's asked her and of course she says she didn't. And maybe the wife's right . . .'

'About her family.'

'Yes.'

'A family of thieves.'

'They think it should have been theirs.'

'Well,' he said, and again, 'Well well.'

'Vell vell,' she mimicked. 'Vot does that mean, Bertholdt?'

He could feel her taking control again—of herself, but also of him. This was what he had resented, this was what had made his life with her difficult. He said, 'It means for example *How interesting.* It means *Does the Herr Professor often take students upstairs?*'

'No, of course he doesn't.'

'And so he doesn't want it known.'

'No.'

'And yet he told you, Sylv.'

She sighed. 'Please don't call me Sylv.'

They were used to the half light now and he stared at her from the shadows, saying nothing. She waited for him to speak. When he didn't she said, 'He told me because he's worried. He needed to talk to someone.'

'That's good. That's so nice. And what did you say, Sylv?'

'Fuck you, Bertholdt.'

He thought she would weep next, but after a moment she said, 'I told him he should tell the police . . .'

'Good advice. But he won't because he wouldn't want his wife to know.'

'She needn't be told. Cops can be discreet.'

'So . . . will he do that?'

She shrugged. 'Not sure. Probably not.'

'Maybe you should tell them yourself.'

She got up abruptly. 'I'm going to bed, Bertie.'

He grinned at her in the gloom. 'Please don't call me Bertie.'

IV.

THE

WINTER OF

DISCONTENT

10.

THE APE,

THE SNAKE AND

THE SILVER FOX

THE NARROW STREET, HARDLY MORE than a one-way passage outside the building which contained Louise's two family apartments, led to a lively and leafy little square surrounded by cafés and shops, and in this area roamed a seemingly deranged elderly woman, possibly only (or also) alcoholic, who, as the day wore on, became less inhibited and more aggressive, shouting at people in a loud, tobacco-ravaged voice that she was hungry, though she didn't appear to be ill-fed, and thirsty. She was sometimes a nuisance around Georges's bar-tabac, but he was always quick to call the local street police, who threatened her with arrest and chased her away. She seemed to become particularly fixed, for several days at a time, on one or another person in the neighbourhood, and lately it had been Max. 'Monsieur, I'm hungry,' she shouted whenever she saw him, and followed him along the street with her hand out, making further appeals which became abuse when there was no response. It was more usual for needy people to sit, heads bowed, a fixed expression of meekness and pain, and perhaps a sign, 'I'M HUNGRY', or even, as Max had seen more than once, misspelled 'I HANGRY', perhaps a genuine mistake, or written thus deliberately to emphasise helplessness, or even a clever pun. Max had been approached once near Saint-Sulpice by a woman of his own age, sober and with such a refined, intelligent face and tidy appearance that when she asked him for a euro he said, without thought, 'Sure . . .' and asked, as he felt in his pockets for his coin purse, 'What's the problem?'

She said, 'I have to sleep in the streets.'

He was shocked. His question had expected some simple, practical explanation—a coin for a telephone booth or parking meter. She saw his surprise and embarrassment. 'It's hard, isn't it?' she said.

He gave her all the euros and smaller coins that slid out of the expensive little eel-skin purse that came from Italy, and hurried on.

Max was sorry for those sleeping rough—and there were a number, too many in this neighbourhood—but he had found, with this madwoman who had now selected him for loud attention, sympathy did not work. Nothing worked except to ignore her and escape. Any engagement at all led only to another and another, each worse, louder, angrier than the one before. A gentle tone was answered with aggression; offers of help enraged her.

It was the evening of 11 November and Max was heading home on foot after a weary commemoration of the 1918 Armistice, involving (slightly puzzling, he had thought) the honouring of a crypt in the Sorbonne Nouvelle's principal courtyard where nine heroes of World War II were interred. The speeches had been long, high-octane French, and by the time it was over he was wanting a rest from the language. He had almost reached the gates to their own courtyard, locked just before nightfall and opened only with an electronic key, when he heard this old harridan coming after him, shouting that there was something she needed. As he reached the gate and touched his key to the electronic pad, she was almost opposite him on the narrow street. He heard her scuttling after him as he pushed the gate open. He knew if she got into the courtyard it would be very difficult to get her out. 'Monsieur, Monsieur' she was yelling, hoarse and insistent. He managed to get in and push the gate shut against its normal slow-paced closure before she could reach him. Then he stood, head down, listening to the abuse as it came to him through the heavy wooden gate, and feeling momentarily that the Paris out there was still Balzac's, or Victor Hugo's, and that he was one of the privileged and therefore guilty. *À bas les aristos!* Was that where he found himself?

It was how he'd felt a few years back when the winter was so cold the homeless were dying in the streets, and the city authorities had issued them with tents and sleeping bags, an improvement on their usual cardboard cartons and ragged blankets. So they had camped in alleys and doorways, over the Métro grilles, even along the bridges, creating anxiety among the well housed, warm indoors, the whole event somehow signalling the unwillingness of the many to care about the few. If there was guilt, Max had thought then, and thought now, he must be one of the guilty. He felt divided against himself—a weightless person, academic, literary, disconnected from reality, lying awake at night hoping to think of how to write a poem (a serious poem, a good one) perhaps about another weightless person, the beautiful Sylvie Renard, or the mysterious Helen White, and unable to invent even a line—while people not far away were sleeping in the streets.

He remembered a poem W.H. Auden had written at the time of his serious commitment to the cause of the Left, which began 'Out on the lawn I lie in bed / Vega conspicuous overhead / In the windless nights of June', and went on to tell of his own and his friends' delicate sensibilities, their 'kindness to ten persons', which the poem implied was trivial compared to the great issues of the time.

At today's Sorbonne ceremony he'd noticed the dome, the clock-face and tower at one end of that magnificent courtyard were unwrapped, after many months of restoration work. And before the ceremony he'd looked in at the refurbished library. In fact the whole institution—the grand halls and marble corridors, the entrances and staircases, the artworks and tapestries—it was all looking magnificent. Marble halls, indeed! And yet it was said to be bankrupt. And the City of Paris, or France itself which just today had claimed a major share in landing a spacecraft on the comet named 67P, after a ten-year pursuit over three million miles, could not afford to do anything for the madwoman still shouting at him on the other side of the gate.

Max unlocked it and pushed twenty euros into her dirty hand with its uncut nails that yesterday, pursuing him, had scratched his arm. It was an amount that might make her day, or it might kill her, and he gave it knowing that anything short of inviting her in to share his apartment was the equivalent of Auden's 'kindness to ten persons'. At least it silenced her, and he retreated behind the gate again, reflecting that even offering to share the apartment, anything short of the Revolution itself, for the Auden of those years would have been unsatisfactory. 'Yesterday all the past, tomorrow perhaps, but *today the Struggle!*' That was the young Auden, before he had given up politics and social issues as too hard and retreated back into the Anglicanism of his childhood.

Indoors Max was extravagantly greeted by unjudging and largely brainless Skipper, and he set about making supper for them both. Skipper could have been the dog, in the squib by Alexander Pope, who said:

> I am his Highness' dog at Kew.
> Pray tell me, Sir, whose dog are you?

But fortunately he was not a proud dog, and would lift a leg with whatever breed of pooch came his way.

•

AFTER THE SUMMER BREAK HELEN had found herself new accommodation in the rue Cardinal Lemoine, not many doors up from a travel agency, Under Hemingway's, so named because Hemingway had lived there when writing *A Moveable Feast*. Helen admired that book, and also the Paris parts of his novel *Fiesta*, though not the man himself, who had liked shooting lions, hooking giant fish, and watching men and bulls killing one another with sharp objects. But *A Moveable Feast* had caught a lovely place at a lovely time. There were unforgettable things in that book—like Scott Fitzgerald's anxieties about satisfying Zelda, his 'mad', and madly talented, wife. And then there was big, bossy Gertrude Stein saying, 'Don't argue with me, Hemingway. It does no good at all.' Helen reread it now and then, and put the rest of Hemingway to one side in her mind, where it seemed most of the world too had put him; while Fitzgerald by contrast was always at the forefront of the world's mind, if only in the latest movie remake of *The Great Gatsby*. But where was Gertrude Stein? Who read her now? She was gone beyond recall. The world had assigned her to a remote shelf of literary history, as Max said his wife's uncle Henri had been shelved in a concrete mausoleum in the cemetery of Montparnasse. You can't argue with that, Stein, Helen told the Gertrude in her head; it does no good at all.

She had arranged her new accommodation through a friend, Maris, a young Brazilian woman who was to share it with her and another, Nina, a Russian. The three were all to help in a café in the little square just up the road, serving at tables and cleaning, which covered most of the cost of their accommodation. It was understood that they would be taking part-time courses during the week. Helen was closer now to the university than she'd been in the rue Parrot; and not quite so poor, because there were always free meals to be had from the café kitchen at times when they were not busy.

She was pleased with herself, especially when Hugh came over for a weekend and she introduced him to her two friends as her fiancé. She was surprised how exciting that seemed. I'm an idiot, she told herself. But Houseboat Hugh—he was so nice, so fond, so civilised and helpful. He didn't seem to mind the uncertainty she had brought into his life.

Her period had come and it was better that she did not have to tell him she was pregnant, which might have upset him. Pregnancy would have been an interesting experience—she had quite liked the idea; but they said it hurt a lot giving birth; and after that you would be stuck with a baby, like a big, noisy doll, getting bigger all the time, and before long walking and talking and probably telling you off—and perhaps even falling into the canal. No, she would be more careful from now on. Fucks for sure, but with care and a condom.

'One day at a time' was the principle she'd learned during her time of enforced hospitalisation; and for the moment one day followed another in an orderly manner, with lithium kept at a level that allowed excitements which were not exactly 'highs', and with Prozac just now and then to protect her from the really bad lows. That, she told Maris and Nina, was her cocktail, her self-medication, and they understood. They knew that a young woman alone in a foreign land had to look after herself. Each had to find her own method, and this was hers.

And so ('one day at a time') this was a few days, a week or so, after the one that had taken her to the Place de Clichy, and coming back to the rue Cardinal Lemoine from an early lecture, she found her flatmates standing out on the street accompanied by two police officers, a man and a woman. She was not to go in; their apartment was being searched. 'Something about a missing painting,' Maris said. 'They seem to think you might have it.'

'Have you?' Nina asked.

'You are Helen White?' the policewoman said. 'Did you remove —I think the word used was "borrow"—a painting from the apartment of . . .' She looked down at her clipboard. 'Professor Louise Simon-Jackson?'

Helen said in English that her French was not very good, and the woman asked the question again, very slowly—did she have an important painting that had been removed from a wall at . . .

No, Helen said, she did not have any paintings.

'You are sure?'

Yes, she was sure.

'If you have it we will find it.'

'Good,' she said in English. And in French, '*Bonne chance.*'

When the three young women were allowed to return to their apartment they found things scattered, opened, thrown about, turned over and ransacked. It was minor wreckage but nothing was broken or damaged. Nothing had been found. The wreckers, it seemed, had been instructed to be gentle, considerate.

'I am sorry for the inconvenience,' the senior officer said. 'This was a matter which required immediate investigation.' To Helen he said, 'You have a locker at the university, Mademoiselle.'

Yes Helen had a locker.

'Could you take me to it, please, and open it in my presence? I will drive you there if you agree. This would be best for you because you have not had time to prepare—you understand?'

Yes, she understood.

'Of course you could refuse, but then . . .'

But no, Helen did not refuse. They could go at once.

They drove to the Sorbonne, no great distance, and he parked in the rue des Écoles. It was a no-parking zone but he left his lights flashing and they went in.

Helen led the way, through a warren of lower corridors to the student lockers, where she opened hers and stood back for him. There was a sweater, a scarf, a pair of running shoes, two packets of tampons and one of condoms, some sketchbooks, and three books, which the officer took out and flicked through, as if some clue might be found there. One was a bright new copy of *Dora Bruder* by Patrick Modiano, still with its purchase print-out from Gibert Joseph inside, and with its red wrap-around declaring '*Prix Nobel de Littérature 2014*'.

'A fine writer,' the officer observed.

'I find him spooky,' Helen said, using the English word.

'What is spooky?'

'Very distinguished,' Helen said.

'Ah yes, distinguished, of course.' And he tried the English word. 'Spooky.'

The other two books were *livres de poche* she had picked up from a second-hand book stall, both Katherine Mansfield—*La Garden-Party*, and *Le Voyage Indiscret*.

'I've seen her grave,' Helen said, as if these were books that needed an excuse. 'It's at Fontainebleau-Avon.'

He nodded, putting them back, locking the little door and returning her key.

'Everything is in order, Madame. Do you wish me to drive you back to your apartment?'

She noticed she was now Madame. No, she thanked him. She preferred to walk.

She went with him back to his flashing car. When he shook her hand and thanked her politely, she asked, 'Why did you search, Monsieur?'

'We act on instruction, of course.'

'Someone must have suggested . . .'

'Yes, that seems to be the case.'

'So . . .' She let him see that she wanted him to tell her more. But he did not know, he said, who had suggested she might have the picture, or why, and if he had known he would probably not have been permitted to tell her.

'I'm sorry,' he said. 'At least it appears the matter is now closed.'

•

SYLVIE WAS IN THE POST Office under the arcades in the rue de Vaugirard, feeling in her handbag for her wallet. It wasn't there. She scrabbled among the contents and then, desperate and flustered, emptied them all on to a little table provided for filling forms and addressing packages. No wallet. She'd had it when she stopped for coffee two blocks away, so had not left it at home. Had it dropped out in the street, or been left at the Café Bonaparte?

Hot in the face, worried not about the cash it contained but about her *carte d'identité*, credit and debit cards, library cards, driver's licence—all the things that would have to be renewed— she began to retrace her steps, first in the Post Office, then slowly along the street.

It began to rain again, and she put up her umbrella. There were short, sharp, chilly wind gusts making navigation among the pedestrian traffic more difficult. She turned into the rue Bonaparte and there in the gutter was a wallet—but not . . . Was it?

She picked it up and checked carefully. The right colour, dark brown, and the right shape, but no, not hers. She looked around but people hurried this way and that, none of them hunting for anything. She held it up above her head as if appealing for a taker. No one even glanced at her, or if they did it was only to turn eyes back to wherever they were going, to whatever they were doing.

She put it into her handbag and continued with her search. When she reached Le Bonaparte, eyes still down, still hunting, she was greeted by a waiter outside under the awning, whose broad smile was good news. 'Madame neglected to pay,' he said. 'But she left her wallet.'

She was profuse in thanks and apologies, explaining that her mind had been on too many other things this morning. And to his suggestion that she should have something to settle the nerves now that she had her wallet and the breakfast rush was over, she said yes please, she would have an infusion, a *tilleul*, and this time she would pay—twice!

So she sat where she had sat less than an hour before, in a corner against the red upholstery and under the bronze bust of the little corporal himself for whom the café was named, and, while she waited for her infusion, took out the wallet she'd found and looked for clues about its owner. There were many. It appeared his name was Leonard Bourguignon de Becker, which sounded rather distinguished, and he lived in the rue Tournefort, right here in the 5th. There were some papers suggesting he had something to do with a committee working to have Nicolas Sarkozy selected as Les Républicains' candidate for the next presidential election. There was a cell-phone number she assumed was his and she called it.

There was something urgent and harassed in the voice that answered, as you might expect a man who had just lost his wallet to sound.

'*Oui?*' he said. And then identified himself. 'Bourguignon de Becker.'

Ah, so he used it all—quite a mouthful. Sylvie went straight to the point. 'Have you lost a wallet, Monsieur?'

'Yes. How did . . . How do you . . .' and so on. Flustered, full of hope and anxiety mixed and shaken.

'I have it.'

'Oh shit thank God thank you . . . Where?'

'The Café Bonaparte. You know it?'

'Of course. Can you wait—if I come at once? It's no distance.'

'Yes. I'm having an infusion, and I have something to read. You can be here in twenty minutes?'

'Of course. Less than that. I would be so grateful, Madame. I'll come at once. What is your name? How will I know you?'

'Sylvie Renard. I'm indoors. Napoléon is looking over my shoulder.'

'Napoléon?'

'His bronze bust.'

'Got it! Of course. You can't imagine what a relief this is . . .'

'Yes I can. I just lost mine and found it.'

'I'm on my way. Don't move.'

So her loss had turned into an adventure, and in the meantime she went on with checking through papers submitted for their conference on poets killed in the Great War. Among them she still had the one Max's friend Helen White had offered on the poetry of Edward Thomas, and Sylvie turned back to it, feeling a mix of curiosity and irritation. Helen was obsessed with certain words, and her paper was constructed around them. One was 'reality'. Thomas had said he was interested, not so much in 'realism' as in reality itself; and Helen had connected this with Wallace Stevens, who had been the one to say that 'reality' was the poet's 'necessary angel'. But there had been, Helen's paper went on, other 'necessary angels' in Thomas's life, the most important being his wife, Helen—and Sylvie could feel how much it pleased Helen White that she shared the name.

With Thomas's poem 'Adlestrop', Helen's paper brought together the place name and the reality. The name itself somehow managed to sound indelibly English, and by that means to accord with, and even perhaps suggest, its own reality—the empty station platform, the willows, the hissing steam and then silence; the grass and the haycocks, the floating clouds and finally a single singing blackbird which became, in the poet's imagination, all the birds of the two counties round about. It was the emphasis on sound and silence in all this that won Sylvie's attention and (though not altogether willing) admiration.

The paper finished by acknowledging that it had offered little on the subject of the war, but that was because Thomas, though he had fought and died in it, had himself said little about it, and his poems had seemed to avoid it. But Helen would finish by letting just one stanza represent the war and Thomas's fate in it:

There is not any book
Or face of dearest look
I would not turn from now
To go to that unknown
I must enter, and leave, alone
I know not how.

The lines were clumsy, but they were very touching, especially when you knew he was about to be killed when he wrote them, and Sylvie was moved. Helen White's paper, if they let her give it, was perhaps wide of the mark, not quite the conventional academic 'thing', but it would be noticed; it would make an impression. Was that what Sylvie wanted? She was not sure whether she had already put Max off including it—and in any case his bizarre adventure with Helen, and the disappearance of the Cézanne, had probably ended any chance that she would be included. Perhaps that was a pity . . .

Sylvie looked up and saw that a man was waiting to catch her attention.

'Bad news?' he said.

'Not at all. Good news in effect. I'm reading a paper offered for an academic conference. When an academic paper almost causes you to shed a tear rather than yawn . . .'

'You know it's good?'

'You know at least it's not the usual run of such things.' She stood up to shake his extended hand. 'Monsieur B de B,' she said.

'Lenny,' he said.

'And I am Sylvie.'

He was tall, well groomed, wearing a well-cut suit of a kind you seldom saw inside the walls of the Sorbonne. He was young, handsome, with wavy dark hair and a moustache. Sylvie thought he looked ready to do whatever was necessary, even something ruthless, to re-elect Nicolas Sarkozy. She regretted the moustache.

He took the chair she pointed to across the table but said he would not have coffee.

She thought, not at once, but as an exchange between them went on, that he passed the test she had for every man within a certain age range. It was nothing, or only a little, to do with looks, or dress, and it was not simply a matter of intelligence. It was, 'Would I go out with him?' and the answer to this crude but crucial question was, 'Yes, I think I might.'

It was an intuitive thing, not a matter of scoring, but it could be broken down into its elements. Certain verbal mannerisms, for example, ruled a candidate out instantly—clichés, male pomposities and insensitivities, especially if they came often. And then physical clumsiness, awkwardness—Sylvie looked for grace of movement: the male as dancer rather than as athlete, though athlete would do. Voice was important—not accent (foreign accents could be charming) but quality, timbre. Bertholdt's was deep, Max's light (and both foreign); they were bass and tenor, but each was in its own way expressive, capable of a certain lyricism; and both sang in tune.

Another test came at close quarters—something to do with pheromones, Sylvie supposed. A man had to smell nice—not of soap or aftershave but of himself. And being older helped: a woman didn't want a partner who related to her as if he were her little brother. Like most men who passed all these tests, both Max and Bertholdt were already married. That was what made life difficult for young women: the world was full of desirable older males already married to desirable women; and this was an especially difficult fact if you had not grown out of the habit of falling in love. Sylvie had been in love with Bertholdt, and more recently with Max. She was willing to acknowledge this as a failing, and told herself she was 'working on it'.

Across the coffee table Lenny Bourguignon de Becker was saying there should be some kind of reward for finding his wallet. He was embarrassed offering this to a woman he could see would not accept—but he was going through the motions. As she shook her head, dismissing it, he said at least he would pay for her *tilleul*.

'And a coffee,' she said. 'Would you?' She explained how in her haste she had left without paying.

Yes of course he would. Yes yes . . . His affirmatives came thick and fast.

'Thank you, that would be very kind.'

He did not seem to her a married man, and this was more or less confirmed when he told her he lived in what he called 'a cupboard' in the rue Tournefort. It was what estate agents called a studio, designed for one.

'That's what I need,' she said. 'A studio in the fifth.' She was not just signalling that their cases were the same—though she knew she was doing that as well. Her attachment to Bertholdt was not destined to last, and where would she go then? She could live at St Germain-en-Laye with her parents, but she did not want that, and probably neither did they. Her 'stuff' was there; but her work was here, in the 5th and the 3rd.

'There are usually one or two vacating in our building,' Lenny said.

Vacating. She didn't like that. It was an example of office-speak, agent-talk, and tending to male self-importance. It went with the suit and the committee to re-elect the dark master of French politics.

'Don't let me detain you,' she said. 'You're going to have a busy life getting Sarko back into the Elysée Palace.'

'We're halfway there—once he becomes the official

Républicains' candidate . . .'

'Then he has to beat Hollande.'

'That's the easy part. The poll-ratings . . .'

'But a week in politics . . .' Sylvie said.

'Is a long time, I know. But Hollande . . .' He shook his head and pulled his mouth down at the corners so the moustache became a protective hedge.

'A lost cause, you think?'

'Don't you?' He got up and reached to shake hands again.

'We shall see,' she said. 'I voted for Hollande and I expect I will again. Au revoir, Monsieur.'

'Au revoir, Sylvie. You have my card there. Keep me in mind if you need a cupboard in the rue Tournefort. I will enquire for you.'

'Thank you. I will.'

And yes, she thought, I will Monsieur Lenny B de B. But first, the hedge should be trimmed.

•

LOUISE WAS CONVINCED NOW—IT WAS her family who had done it. Their circle of university friends had heard about the picture, some had seen it, but beyond that it was not known at all, hardly spoken about, received no public attention. And only the family would have had a motive and wanted it so much. It was even possible Uncle Henri's daughters and his widow, who were close in age, had put aside their hatred for one another and worked together. They could have hired a professional. She knew, and not just from her recent reading of Simenon, that such things were possible, such people existed. There was a whole underworld out there of cunning thieves and con-men ready to do pretty much anything for money. The security code could have been cracked. That would not have been a problem for a real pro. And bribing the concierge was a common shortcut. Not that Monsieur Ferney would have been easily persuaded. On the whole he was a loyal and honest retainer. But, if you believed Simenon, there was nothing a concierge would not do if the bribe was big enough and the consequences not too dire.

The picture would have to be kept hidden, the theft kept secret; but there would have been such pleasure for them in scoring over her, defeating her, avenging her courtroom triumph over the late, great Henri, older son and family scion. They might hide it anywhere—in a bank vault somewhere in the city, perhaps. She had told Captain Olivier that it would be hidden in the depths of the château, and she had pleaded with him to order a search there. But on reflection she had to acknowledge that this was unlikely: too obvious; too easily discovered. And the château was not kept warm and dry in winter. The picture, kept there, would deteriorate very quickly.

It could be anywhere by now—in Switzerland, for example, in whichever bank one or the other used for their secret numbered accounts. As she thought of this she imagined disagreements about whose bank, the daughters' or the widow's, would be used. But they would have had to be on their best behaviour with one another. Quarrels, disagreements, would endanger their whole project.

There had been that brief excitement when it was thought it might have been stolen by one of Max's students. Louise's hopes had been raised, but only briefly. Captain Olivier had acted very quickly on that suggestion, wherever it had come from—no doubt because there were not the legal obstacles there would have been to any attempt to question the family or search their premises. The English girl (said to be bipolar and on medication) had been questioned and her apartment searched. They had even made her open her locker at the Sorbonne. Nothing had come of it—of course. It had been a diversion; a case of following a wrong lead. Louise felt she had known that all along.

It was sad. She would never see the picture again. Those hated women would make sure of that—even though they were not able to see much of it themselves. Now, she told herself, she must ensure that she did not give them the satisfaction of seeing that she cared.

There was a problem about insurance. Because the picture had never been authenticated, it was going to be impossible to get reasonable compensation for the loss—and it seemed likely that months, years probably, would pass before the matter was settled and anything paid. But Louise was taking her own revenge now. She had never doubted the authenticity of the revered 'picture'. Now she was allowing in her statement for the possibility that it had all been family myth rather than family history. Cézanne might have been the forebear's friend, or acquaintance, or whatever. That did not make the picture his work. And who exactly was this famous forebear? Was he the one who had been Flaubert's doctor, or another? If it was a copy, it was an exceptionally good one; even brilliant. But, until it reappeared, no one would ever be certain about it.

Louise was taking comfort now in her forthcoming Pléiade edition. Already she was receiving renewed attention and respect. TV and radio interviews were booked, newspaper reviews promised, and a launch planned. It was time for her to move away from that old, rather shop-soiled identity as the daughter of a distinguished French family, and stand in her own light as academic, editor and teacher, senior Professor at '*l'Université Sorbonne Nouvelle, Paris 3*'.

She had bought a very good Matisse lithograph, one of just 250 signed (in fact initialled 'H.M.') by the artist and authenticated.

Already it was on the wall where the picture had been; and already the family (and Gina) were learning to refer to it, not as 'the picture', but as 'the Matisse'.

•

MAX SAID TO HIS CLASS, 'As you can see I've run over time on Faulkner and now, since this is our last scheduled lecture before the Christmas break, there are only a few minutes left to say something about the last book on our list, Nabokov's *Lolita*.'

There was a rustle of paper and scratching of pens and biros as they turned a new page in their notebooks and made headings.

'There's so much to say about *Lolita*,' he went on. 'An unfashionable subject—paedophilia—and treated by Nabokov in a way which would not now be condoned. Distasteful when it was written—much more so now, I think, in a world so aware of it as a fact and a crime. And this is a comic novel, a fact which seems improper. It's also a tragedy. A satire on America, and yet a lament for its dark "hero" and first-person narrator, Humbert Humbert, whose passion for his child-love, Lolita, is written out with so much fine feeling, so much European sophistication, so much stylistic panache.'

Max left his notes and stepped around in front of the lectern so he would be closer to his students and could read their faces.

'But I want to suggest an odd angle on this novel. A Paris angle. It's very much, very consciously, an American book by a Russian exile who was trying, he said, to turn himself into an American writer. And *Lolita* did that for him. It made him famous there, a bestseller, able soon to leave the States, leave his work there as a university professor, and spend the rest of his life as a writer in Europe.

'So much about Nabokov is strange,' Max said. 'Some of you

will have seen those photographs of him armed with a net, going into the American woods in pursuit of butterflies and moths. It's like a little parody, or a caricature, of the paedophile in pursuit of what Nabokov calls the "nymphet"—the nubile just pre-pubescent girl, seducible, or herself the seducer, with her . . .'

He paused a moment, finding the right page in the copy of the novel still in his hand. 'Here it is: with her "fey grace", her "elusive, shifty, soul-shattering, insidious charm".

'I don't suppose Nabokov invented the word "nymphet" but it would have pleased him that it was close to the word "nymphalid", which is a kind of butterfly.

'And yet the book began here in Paris. Nabokov recounts in a note written in 1956 that what he calls "the first little throb of *Lolita*" came to him in 1939 or 1940 when he read a newspaper story about an ape in the Jardin des Plantes being coaxed by a scientist to do a drawing with charcoal, and finally producing a sketch that seemed to be an image of the bars of its cage. This, Nabokov says, was "the first shiver of inspiration" for a story written in Russian, which had the basic elements of what became the novel. He thought the story didn't work and abandoned it; but almost ten years later, in New York, he says, "the throbbing, which had never quite ceased, began to plague me again"—and so the writing of the story began again, this time in English, growing into the very substantial book it now is—not ending as the original story did with the rejected paedophile's suicide, but with his—should we call it?—"success", lasting over several years, and ending with his murder of a rival who has stolen the incomparable and beloved Lolita away from him.

'What is the connection between an ape doing a charcoal drawing of the bars of its cage, and the story which became *Lolita*? Why was there that "throb", that "shiver of inspiration"—and why did the "throbbing" stay with him for ten years? There's a mystery here, and I put it together in my mind with the quality of the writing—because this novel is unquestionably a stylistic *tour de force*. At intervals throughout the book you feel the pressure rise as Humbert gives vent to his feelings for the child, his aching love for her, and his irrepressible lust. Nabokov has entered imaginatively and so completely into Humbert's feelings for his victim, it's hard not to see it, or to *feel* it, as having a kind of purity—or perhaps, since it isn't pure, and even Humbert condemns himself and his actions, then let's call it true: true love, but impure; authentic love, but unacceptable and even distasteful.

'This is a book about America—and in part a satire on America's post-Second-World-War teenage culture. It's a book like its almost exact contemporary, Jack Kerouac's *On the Road*, about being on the move. It's about motels, cars and gasoline, advertising hoardings, and cinemas—Lolita is addicted to the worst kinds of Hollywood movies. It's about brash, vulgar, successful, affluent, commercial 1950s America: hideous décor, chewing gum, burgers and popular culture. Much of what Kerouac celebrates, Nabokov deplores; but they are recording the same social facts, and exploiting the same freedom from sexual restraint and from the rules and restrictions of middle America.

'That, surely, is how the ape here in Paris's Jardin des Plantes figured as Nabokov's inspiration, and at least two momentary glimpses of Humbert as the ape survive in the finished text. On page forty-two of the new Penguin edition we read, "A polka-dotted black kerchief tied around her chest hid from my aging ape-eyes, but not from the gaze of young memory, the juvenile breasts I had fondled one immortal day." And ten pages on: "Perhaps my ape-ear had unconsciously caught some slight change in the rhythm of her respiration." It is ape-eyes that see Lolita, and ape ears that hear her breathing. So the idea that first set the writing in motion remains hidden away in the finished form. Humbert Humbert is the ape behind the bars of middle-class propriety— and so is Nabokov. The throb that lasted ten years was of a lust in Nabokov which he wanted to be free to express, even though he knew it was unacceptable and if acted upon in reality rather than fiction would put him behind bars. After ten years he found a way to release it; the ape remained behind bars, but the novel *Lolita* liberated its author from the horrible prison of America.

'And there is another Parisian aspect to the novel. Nabokov couldn't at first find an American publisher willing to take the book, but he found one here in Paris—the Olympia Press. So the book which began here returned to be published; and from that start it went, as we say, "global".

'Well . . .' He returned to the lectern and scooped up his notes. 'Those are some random thoughts. I warn you, though, *Lolita* is in many ways an unsavoury book. Take that for granted, and then try to decide whether you think it's also a work of genius. I wish you joy of it, as the clown wishes Cleopatra "joy of the worm"— by "worm" meaning the asp she's about to put to her breast to kill herself.

'And do enjoy your Christmas break, all of you. I look forward to seeing you in the New Year.'

•

IT HAD BEEN AN IMPULSE. Pure impulse. Helen loved that painting so much, its greens, its yellow-greens, its splash of orange, its overhanging trees and sinister pool. And the air of mystery, perhaps of death, death by drowning, that hung over it, and emanated from it.

She'd wanted it, and not just for herself, or perhaps not for herself at all, but for him, Max, the one who, just before she'd taken it down from the wall, had made her so happy. Euphoric. Ah, the dangers of euphoria, how well she knew them and how little she cared when they were upon her. And yes, that was it! Why not?—for him—for Max, who was not in love with her because he was in love with Sylvie Renard, but that didn't matter.

And the painting—it was his, rightfully. She thought so. She felt it—knew it. It was something to do with the spirit of the thing, which made her think of a dead body (perhaps one of the sisters) and the mysteriousness of death. This was not a gloomy thought—not at all. It was heroic—how life stopped, and for a moment everything stopped, perfect, beautiful, and the great painter had caught it, the moment of death before the loveliness of everything went, passed, 'passed away' out into silence and decomposition and nothingness.

Max's French wife, the important one, Professor Louise Simon-Jackson, with her commission for that Pléiade edition and her proofs from Gallimard—she would understand none of this. How could she, when she had tipped Max out of the nest, had sent him downstairs, had decommissioned him, as if he had no rights at all. Helen had been able to feel her presence, even on that day with Max at Fontainebleau-Avon; even on the day in Paris when Louise had been far away. At such a distance from him, away on holiday on the Italian Riviera, Louise still ruled his life. He might be in love with Sylvie, and entertained by Helen, but he was ruled by Louise. Louise the dark force; Louise the snake. That was true, and it was wrong. It was what needed to change. Something should happen to make it change.

Her eyes had gone back to the painting. Who were the sisters and what was their story? She thought one sister might have drowned the other. There was an English or Scots ballad like that. The murdered one sings from the pond, 'There sits my sister who drownèd me.' Was that the story, or a story like it, that had inspired Cézanne?

She had reached up and taken the picture by its frame, tried it. It was not heavy and had lifted easily off its two hooks.

An impulse, that was all, but it had seemed a right one, a good one. The canvas in its light frame could be made to slide so easily into her carry-all with a sketchbook on either side for protection. That it went in unresisting, and sat comfortably under her arm and against her thigh as if it belonged there—that had confirmed it was the right thing to do. What would she do with it? She did not know, would not think about that yet—only knew that she had yielded, in her euphoria, to the demand the picture itself, and the painter through the picture, had made of her—a demand which, even after these nervous weeks of expecting trouble, she still could not feel had been wrong.

Since her day at Fontainebleau-Avon she had looked often in the library at Katherine Mansfield's journals and she had found there, and copied, something which was almost a description of the picture.

> The mind I love must have wild places, a tangled orchard
> in heavy grass, an overgrown little wood, the chance of a
> snake or two, a pool that nobody has fathomed the depth
> of, and paths threaded with flowers.

It was eerie that she and Max should have seen the place where this woman died, the very stairs on which her final haemorrhage had occurred, and had seen, even, her grave, so close to the grave of the Master, Gurdjieff, their instructor, hers and Katherine's. Helen felt even now the *Kaife* of the great man—and she still had the fine yellow-and-gold cotton handkerchief she had laid out on his gravestone that day. He would instruct her. He would know what she should do.

Someone had given the police her name. She did not want to think it was Max. She did not believe he would have done that. He had said if she had the picture she should tell him and he would help her return it—in secret, anonymously. But he must have told someone else about her having been with him to the upstairs apartment. Not his wife—he would not have wanted Louise to know about that day. But Sylvie—he might have told her because he was in love with her. When you were in love with someone you might tell them anything. Sylvie Renard. Renard was French for fox. She was the Silver Fox. She might have done it.

Helen knew she could still trust Max. But, if she went to him now and told him where the picture was, he would find a way to make sure it went straight back to his wife, and Helen did not want that. She wanted to take the painting away from Louise as she felt Louise was taking Max from others—from Sylvie, from herself.

Tonight, and every night until she had the answer, she would sleep with her head on the yellow handkerchief she had laid out on Gurdjieff's grave, and try to dream of him. Gurdjieff and Katherine Mansfield: they would tell her what she must do.

11.

JE SUIS

CHARLIE

THE DECEMBER WIND FROM THE north-east skipped quickly across Scandinavia, treating Stockholm politely as the great and the good gathered there to award this year's Nobel Prizes, and to hear Patrick Modiano of France say thank you, suggesting that his trade was that of a spy on the conversations of others, and that, though the blank page terrified him, the need to speak and be heard was compelling. The same wind skimmed over Germany, and seemed to save more than a fair share of unpleasantness to punish the pride of Paris that had gone before the fall of its leaves, already swept away from the tree-lined boulevards, and only lingering in the memory of the Luxembourg Gardens. In Max's sheltered courtyard it turned random sniper and picked off one by one the last poor, cringing survivors. But now, by way of substitute or compensating alternative, the Paris trees had taken on lights. All along the Champs-Élysées they shifted from white to violet to red. The Town Hall blazed. On the main plaza in front of Notre-Dame an enormous decorated conifer had appeared, a gift from Moscow, a coal of fire perhaps because France, in protest at Russia's military activities in Ukraine, was delaying delivery of two warships. Nine more grand trees, gifts from France to itself, had been set up in front of the Panthéon. Around the Place de l'Opéra and along the Boulevard Haussmann—in fact in all the deciduous trees of inner Paris—white lights sprang to life along bare branches, while in its churches innumerable versions of the baby Jesus, some white, some black or brown, were visited by three wise men bearing gifts. Indifferent, the Seine flowed on as it had done before the Christmas festival ever broached its banks or adorned its shores. At the Sorbonne Nouvelle last classes were given before the break that would begin on 19 December and last until 5 January.

And in the world? In Pakistan the Taliban gunned down 140 children in a school. The Paris cartoonist, Charb, had said 'The pen is mightier than the sword of Islam.' In principle, maybe—must be!—but in the short term the innocent died.

In Washington and Havana, Barack Obama and Raoul Castro announced a rapprochement between their countries which sent Fox News and the Republican Party into overdrives of outrage. In Washington a committee of Democrats had released their findings on the CIA's 'enhanced interrogations' during the last Bush presidency—simulated drowning, anal 'feeding', locking suspects in coffin-size boxes for hours and days, hanging them by the wrists for similar periods, or subjecting them to intolerable noise and light. You could review these matters quickly—even the case of the one who died of hypothermia after five days chained to a concrete floor—and dismiss them, accepting the assurances that they were 'not torture', that they had saved lives and cost Bin Laden his; or, on the other hand, you could let your imagination linger there. But either way, a short shrug or a lingering wince, what then? This was Paris (or it was London or New York, Johannesburg or Sydney or Auckland), it was December and rushing on towards Christmas. There were presents to buy, and a life to be lived. Maybe there had been unwarranted embraces that had made you think briefly of Gatsby yearning towards the green light across the water that signalled Daisy and his dream. Maybe on the other hand you knew where yearning ended and reality began. Maybe you had been estranged from your spouse, and wondered now whether the current improvement was to be confirmed or reversed. Maybe you were preparing for a *journée d'études* next summer on poetry and death in World War I, but hoping first to finish the writing of a little book on Lessing and Naipaul that a very few tweaks and repairs might make 'perfect'. Maybe your 'mad' friend, the one you had said might be your Muse, had stolen your wife's unauthenticated master-work—and maybe not. And what of the young woman of the expensive shoes and colourful silk scarves, the inter-galactic anxieties and the delicate keyboard fingers? What of her gruff German lover, whose version of Strindberg's *The Ghost Sonata* was earning plaudits? Life, as it always did, went on. Its map was enormous, even infinite (the choice between limit and no limit was yours), Space was vast and Time would not wait.

•

IN THE DOWNSTAIRS APARTMENT THERE were some DVDs of old movies that belonged to the time when they had had a tenant there. Max riffled among them looking for something to take his mind off his book, off his anxiety about Helen and 'the picture', about Sylvie and the conference, and chose one that was ten years old, *36 Quai des Orfèvres*. The choice was not random. He knew it was a cop story, and that it was dark and violent. To accompany him while he watched, he chose a bottle of Côtes du Rhône from the room down there now used as their cellar.

France ten years ago had been noted for humane movies, sometimes metropolitan but often rural, realistic about human folly, whimsical, often funny, with good feeling, good food and wine, and with charm and intelligence. Maybe *36 Quai des Orfèvres* was one of the signals of a change, a French attempt to match Hollywood in violent drama and edge-of-the-seat action. Daniel Auteuil was the good guy, Gérard Depardieu, his hair dyed ginger, the bad one.

But whatever its place in the history of cinema, there was something especially French about it that made Max watch in a mood of gloomy self-punishment and recognition. Auteuil and Depardieu were in love with the same woman—but that, and her death, were incidental. Auteuil was head of the Search and Action Squad, Depardieu head of the Anti-Crime Unit. Their chief was about to retire. They were exactly equal in distinction and ranking. There was a violent gang operating in Paris, robbing armoured cars transporting cash between banks. The minister had demanded that these murderous robbers be stopped. Whichever of our two principal characters, the good or the bad, succeeded in this, would win promotion to the top job.

It was this image of a strict hierarchy, the influence within it of the minister, and the competition for the top job, that seemed so French—all of that together with the fact that what seemed so structured and formalised was also, under the surface, corrupt. One of these two men had to win, and when he did the fact that he had cheated (both would cheat) would be covered over and never mentioned. Apart from the extreme violence, it might have been the Sorbonne.

Max, having drunk more than his usual modest intake of the Côtes du Rhône, went to bed, slept at once and heavily, and woke at 3 a.m., thirsty, and struggling with one further idea which might bring his book to a ringing conclusion. He should write it down or it would be forgotten. He took a few sips of water from the glass beside his bed and felt around in the dark for the torch, the pen and the black Sorbonne Nouvelle notebook he kept there, but could not find them.

He began to repeat the idea to himself so it would not be lost—then fell, suddenly, as if backwards over a cliff, into a black hole.

When he woke next it was early morning, and he was surfacing from a dream that was also a memory of his early days in Paris. He was somewhere in the rue des Écoles with Louise, telling her that her young brother had done well in his baccalaureate exams and had won a scholarship. In the dream he had a cell phone, which he could not have had at the time—and as he recognised this he remembered that Louise did not have a younger, or any, brother. But the 'truth' was not important. There were embraces—it was a warm dream, and he left it reluctantly. As he woke himself up and moved to get out of bed, he saw the black notebook on the floor, and struggled to remember the idea that had come to him in the night.

•

CHRISTMAS CAME, THE WEATHER MILDER than usual, and there was the business of the tree, the decorations, the presents, the children's inexhaustible clamour for everything and the pleasure of satisfying them; all the old nonsense again that seemed right because it was 'normal' and because it could be done, not without twinges of guilt and anxiety about the big unequal world out there where affluence was a fact for some and a dream for many—the good/bad world of 'Nothing to be done about it, alas!' So it was best to make the most of the festival, to enjoy it, and even (for resisting/unresisting Max) to affirm the Church's part in it, the celebration of the birth of the holy Child.

Max moved—had been invited to move—upstairs for Christmas with the family. He and Louise shopped together, bought presents for the children (including a cell phone for Julie and a skateboard for Jean-Claude), and slept in the same bed—'properly', as Gina reported to Georges, 'like a knife and a fork in the same drawer'. They went as a family to midnight mass at the church of Saint-Étienne-du-Mont. They sang together and were happy, all four of them in tune, and once or twice, when Max was invaded by a memory of schooldays as a chorister, in harmony. Louise bought Max a gold ring. He had never worn one, but put this one on and liked it—the feel of it, the look of it. He showed her his owl tattoo without explaining how or why it came about, and she did not enquire—just told him she liked it, it was pretty and yet discreet, and she thought she might do the same. He took her to the little shops in the rue du Cherche-Midi that Sylvie had recommended and bought her shoes. Louise had not usually worn such heels, but she tried them on. Her ankles were good and her calves neat, and she liked them. Returning there alone, he bought her the kind of silk *foulard* Sylvie had bought for the opera, in lovely colours, and so delicate in texture it was a sort of airy nothing, weightless.

Then January arrived, and the new year, 2015, swept in with fierce winds and snow drifts. The puddles of Paris froze hard and the trees waved at the world their stark arms, their creaking or silent signals. Parisians stayed indoors, or hurried between one door and the next, while mysteriously, like flies in winter, the homeless stayed commendably out of sight.

Among the presents Louise gave Max there was a new novel by Michel Houellebecq, called *Submission*. It was not due for publication until 7 January, but she had an advance copy for review, sent by its publisher, Flammarion. Max read it and was, he told her, caught somewhere between discomfort and disbelief. Houellebecq, the writer who had previously had to take cover for dismissing Islam as 'the stupidest religion', now seemed to take it very seriously, and was even able to imagine a future (the one outlined in the novel, set in 2022) where a Muslim Brotherhood Party would be strong enough to win a French election. Running neck-and-neck with Marine Le Pen's National Front, the Brotherhood's charismatic leader, Ben Abbes, forms an alliance with a weak socialist leader to defeat Le Pen and form a new government, with himself as president.

Soon (as the novel continued) Ben Abbes has persuaded the European Union to admit not only Turkey, but Algeria, Morocco and Tunisia to membership. There are indications that Sharia law will soon be introduced in France.

The principal character, François, is a lecturer at the Sorbonne, an expert on the life and fiction of the late-nineteenth-century writer Joris-Karl Huysmans. In parallel with France itself, the Sorbonne is taken over by an Islamist president; and by the end of the story François has earned the right to continue as a professor, but only by converting to Islam.

Were you meant to read this, Max asked himself, as serious prognostication, or just as a 'What if?' and a political entertainment? As prediction it could be dismissed; but as a 'What if' it exercised and troubled the Christian-atheist mind.

SYLVIE MET LENNY—MONSIEUR B-DE-B AS she thought of him—by the fountain at the entrance to the modern building, all glass and steel and artful imitation, on the rue Tournefort, in which he had secured a studio apartment for her only a few doors from his own. She needed this. Bertholdt, who had gone back to Berlin to have Christmas with his family, had completed his contract with Canal and would be terminating his lease on the apartment in the rue de Vaugirard. He would be back in Paris soon, but only briefly, to wind up his affairs and pack his things for transport home. He wanted their farewells, his and Sylvie's, to be amiable, he said, not to leave a deep scar, or even a bad taste.

Bertholdt, it seemed, had known about her affair with Max, and when she told him about it he had reacted without much surprise and little anger. But he seemed to imagine it much more significant than it had been in reality. She didn't correct that. She allowed him to think it had gone on longer and cut deeper. Her pride required it. She didn't tell him how much had been fantasy, her own but Max's too.

Bertholdt wanted them to have an excellent farewell dinner at a restaurant of her choosing, and she intended to enjoy that, and to take him somewhere in Paris he'd never been before, not expensive necessarily, but special. She was working on it, intending to be especially nice to him, surprise him and make him sorry to be leaving Paris and sad to be leaving her.

And meanwhile there was Lenny. In the street now, while the little fountain splashed down into its icy pool, she turned her attention to Monsieur B-de-B. He would have to help her forget Bertholdt, who would have the advantage of absence to make the heart grow fonder, and to forget Max, who would have the advantage of proximity and that nice natural smell his body had at close quarters. And there was still the project she and Max would have to work on together commemorating French and British poets killed in what he liked to call Wobbly Wobbly One . . .

Even the thought of that Wobbly Wobbly One, its quirky pointlessness, its absurdity, stopped her short. That was Max. Couldn't she just focus on his Englishness, his silliness, and stop finding it endearing? That shouldn't be so hard, should it?

But the job ahead for Lenny was considerable; she knew that and fortunately he did not.

Lenny had trimmed his moustache. It was now a modest mo, but still a mo, and unwelcome. He had also, she thought, standing close to him and sniffing discreetly, within the last half hour sprayed himself after showering, so he smelled of something scented but with a male orientation—the odour equivalent perhaps of the taste of a fine, light Greek wine, with something of lemon, something of eucalypt, and the merest dash of kerosene; and this strange, to Sylvie unattractive, odour was emerging through the folds of a heavy overcoat and scarf.

No, Lenny, she wanted to tell him, this would not do. She was going to have to train him, teach him how to dress stylishly but less formally, and to stop perfuming himself. Could she also teach him to shift Leftward in politics without compromising his work for the dark master of the Right, Nicolas Sarkozy? And to care about climate change? Could she introduce him seriously to the big world of books? And would he listen if she told him about quarks, and black dwarfs, and the two trillion galaxies? There was so much to be done with Lenny B de B. He stood before her now like the potter's clay, or the chef's ingredients, or the uncut diamond on which the jeweller must go to work.

All this lay ahead—demanding, even daunting, but exciting.

And at the same time she would have to be working also on herself. Could she learn just, slowly, to love him without first falling—crashing—in love? It seemed unlikely—even the falling seemed unlikely—but she was an optimist by nature and willing to try.

'You're not Catholic are you, Lenny?' she asked, taking him by surprise.

'Catholic? No, Jewish, actually. On my mother's side. What about you?'

'Oh yes, I'm Catholic,' she said. And then, 'Regrettably.'

•

LECTURES HAD NOT BEGUN FOR either Louise or Max. On the morning of 7 January, publication day for Michel Houellebecq's novel, they took Skipper for a walk, delivered the children to the house of friends, and stopped for coffee in the Place Saint-Sulpice. Louise was currently reading the final draft print-out of Max's book. She had her notes with her, with comments to offer and a few minor corrections to suggest. He copied what she had to say into his own notebook, and was grateful. She assured him his 'lit crit', as he called it, was of exceptional quality. The little book, she said, was destined for success.

Returning to the apartment they saw Houellebecq interviewed on *Télématin*, looking ravaged by nicotine, alcohol and perhaps (Max thought) narcotics; but his appearance might have been no more than a style, a way of self-presentation. It went with the character of François in the novel, whose favourite medicine (taken in large doses) was Calvados, and who expressed gratitude to his penis as the only organ that had not presented itself to his consciousness through pain.

The interview was interspersed with reviews of *Submission*

from the day's papers, and extracts from these reviews were read. Mostly reviewers were outraged by what the novel seemed to be proposing—an Islamist future for France. The satirical magazine *Charlie Hebdo* was shown greeting the new publication with a caricature of Houellebecq on its cover, saying '2015 I lose my teeth, 2022 I do Ramadan'.

Houellebecq shrugged most of this off. Yes his teeth were a problem. He was glad there was so much interest in his new work. He hoped that the attention would become more serious as time went by; more thoughtful, more analytical.

It was early afternoon when the news reported a jihadist attack on the offices of *Charlie Hebdo*. Twelve, including the editor, had been shot dead. The attackers had identified themselves as representing ISIS and, for the moment at least, had escaped shouting, 'We have avenged the prophet Mohammad', and 'God is great'.

Louise was frightened. 'I'm scared, Max,' she said, and phoned the children at their friends' house to tell them she would be coming at once to bring them home.

It was said that Michel Houellebecq had cancelled all publicity engagements for his new book and had taken refuge somewhere in rural France.

•

HELEN WHITE WAS BOOKED ON the Eurostar departing Gare du Nord at 11.13 in the morning. Hugh Pennington would be waiting at St Pancras to help her with her luggage and they would go on together to Oxford to set up house—to set up houseboat—together. It was all agreed and arranged. She was not sorry about Paris. It had taught her a lot about herself, and other people, and life, and how a person with a devil on her shoulder could cope with all of these; but she had not discovered what that sentence by Derrida which had brought her here meant. She could still repeat it and, if she let it, it could torment and puzzle her: 'We are dispossessed of the longed-for presence in the gesture of language by which we attempt to seize it.' Max Jackson had become 'the longed-for presence' and she was now putting the Channel between them. *La Manche*, the French called it: the sleeve. No more of the madness of Max. The Chunnel was to put them asunder, and her ankle owl was to be her only memento. She'd said *adieu* to him that morning, with the Cézanne tucked secretly under her arm; not *au revoir* but *adieu*, and by now he would know she had meant it. He had rejected her paper on Edward Thomas— or perhaps it was the Silver Fox who had done that. Whichever: Helen was tired of Thomas and done with Derrida. Maximus and the Silver Fox could keep their dead-soldier poets. She was going back to Houseboat Hugh, who was safe and kind, dependable and unmarried, who studied science and played rugby and the violin, and who loved her and had played *Greensleeves* one summer night, and was consequently her fiancé! How nice was that, how absolutely nifty? She had caught this morning morning's minion and would walk abroad in a shower of all her days.

So with the words of sad Father Gerard and forever-drunk Dylan still ringing in the ears of her mind, she said extravagant fond farewells to her two friends, Brazilian Maris and Russian Nina, hugged them and was hugged, with promises to meet again somewhere in this world or the next, and meanwhile, this side of heaven, to exchange emails and texts and even perhaps old-fashioned postcards and letters, with postage stamps in brightest colours . . .

A taxi had been ordered and was waiting.

IN THE NEXT DAYS THERE were more deaths, among them the two who had carried out the initial attack on the offices of *Charlie Hebdo*. Now there was to be a march in Paris. It would be huge— the numbers might exceed a million, two million. Président Hollande would be at the front, and there would be forty 'world leaders' alongside him. The slogan there, and throughout France and beyond, was to be '*Je suis Charlie*'—I am Charlie. Everyone in the Western world wanted to rally for freedom of speech. Everyone wanted to be Charlie.

Democrats and autocrats, progressive and repressive, they were all to be out there, to be seen *being Charlie*, showing themselves, proclaiming their credentials by saying no to saying no, though at home most of them said 'no' most of the time. But never mind. 'Man, proud man, dressed in a little brief authority' was seeing, and seizing, the opportunity to be seen in a good light. Hollande had for the moment cast off the shadows of those three women, Ségolène, Trierweiler and Julie Gayet, and looked to all the world like the statesman he had all this time wanted to be. He was speaking with dignity and acting with authority. Sarkozy, Le Pen too, fumed and for the moment had no choice but to march in step.

It was the kind of rare unanimity that brings a choking throat and tears of togetherness. Max was moved by it, and yet resistant. 'It's such bullshit,' he told Louise, even though he wept. When he heard that Tony Blair was to take part he said he would not join in.

Louise reasoned with him. This was a moment of history that Julie and Jean-Claude should be able to remember, and to tell others about later: 'We were there, in Paris, the eleventh of January, 2015. We took part.'

'And it's a good cause, Maximus.'

So warm coats and hats, scarves and gloves, had been put on and now, bundled up, the family was heading towards the Seine, knowing they would never reach the heart of the action, that the head of the march (those forty 'world leaders' pushing, elbowing one another aside to be visible to the cameras and seen at home) would be long gone before they crossed to the Right Bank where most of it was going on. But they were sharing the feeling of this enormous crowd, the excitement, the togetherness. *Je suis Charlie.* Just as they had sung together on Christmas Eve, so they marched together now, and were French, and were Charlie, all four of them—and Johnny and Julie had made signs to say so and were holding them aloft.

The crowds grew denser, louder, sometimes alarming. Parents and children hung on to one another's hands and overcoats, the parents shouting to 'stay together', the children, excited, pleased to be out in it. They were making slow progress, but there was no need to get anywhere in particular, because they were *in* it, part of the *tout le monde*, the 'all the world' that was Paris on this day. 'Today,' François Hollande was saying, 'Paris is the centre of the world.'

They were in the rue Monsieur-le-Prince—one of those streets which divide long-ways, with a high and a lower pavement and the roadway between—up on the elevated part, with the crowd filling the whole street below. Stalled there, Max saw that down in the chaos of the roadway Sylvie Renard was struggling through with a clear direction, a clear purpose, checked at intervals, but moving forward, her right arm trailing behind her, her hand gripping the wrist of a young man. From above not much could be seen of him, but Max noted that there were thick, tight, glossy curls and a moustache. That would have to go, surely. Sylvie had a thing about moustaches of every kind; and as he remembered this Max felt a flood of the old affection for her. Quicksilver Sylvie. How he loved her!

'It's like the end of *Les Enfants du Paradis*,' he shouted at Louise, but she shook her head, unable to hear him for the noise. And, when he looked again, his 'Garance' had vanished into the crowd.

•

THE TAXI HAD TAKEN HELEN first to the rue Parrot, where the concierge of the apartment block she'd lived in last summer was waiting for her, as promised, with the yellow-striped hold-all which had once contained a baguette and the picnic lunch she and Max had shared at Fontainebleau-Avon. She gave the concierge twenty euros and asked him to promise he would tell anyone who enquired that he had not seen her and did not know where she was now living, but that he believed she had gone to Canada. When he assured her he would do this, even if it was the police who asked the questions, she gave him another thirty.

At a little gadget shop nearby, which she knew very well, she bought the cheapest of cell phones.

'It's not a very good one,' the young man behind the counter said, his voice lowered so the owner would not hear him. 'It won't do any tricks . . .'

But she did not want tricks from it; did not want anything at all apart from its appearance. It should look like a cell phone, and it did. That was all she wanted. No reason to pay for tricks. The cell phone was itself the trick; it was the signal, the signifier (as Derrida would say); it was the trigger. It might survive the next few hours but the chances were that it would not. It was to be seen, not to function, and she would not even switch it on.

Back in the taxi and seated behind the driver, she stuffed a newspaper, a heavy book, and two slim insulated wires, one red one black, around the slim package already contained in the yellow-striped bag, pulling the wires up so they were just visible, seeming to come up and return down without a break. Finally she placed the cell phone at the top so that, with the bag slightly open, it could be seen. She punched open, and put on, the straw hat with a very broad brim and red-ribbon trimming which she had been keeping squashed among her things. At the Gare du Nord she paid the driver, adding a modest tip. He helped her pile up a few extra items on top of her wheeled luggage and set her off towards the Eurostar departures.

The timing was good, and she was able to sit for a few minutes rearranging her luggage, and then, on her feet again, to wheel it, keeping her head down, into the lines, shepherded by heavily armed police, up the escalator, through passport control, and into the waiting area.

She did not remove the hat until the train was well on its way, skimming through the lovely French countryside towards Pas-de-Calais and the tunnel. The hat would be gone when she got out at St Pancras, left in one of the train's WCs several cars along from the one in which she was sitting in a seat, second class but numbered and reserved.

The only thing she had left behind in Paris, apart from Max himself, was the yellow-striped picnic bag he had liked so much. She had left it leaning against a wall in the Gare du Nord, looking, she thought as she cast a last brief glance back at it, like someone pretending indifference, faking it, lolling there, lounging and dangerous. What a pity it couldn't have a thin cigarette dangling from the corner of its mouth.

In the urgency of the crowded concourse it had been easy to leave it there without drawing attention to herself. Everyone was busy. Everyone was nervous because of the recent killings and the possibility of more. People did not look at one another; but it would not be long before someone noticed a bag.

Maybe 'the picture', the gorgeous Cézanne she had loved so much, would be discovered, identified by the police, and returned to Professor Louise Simon-Jackson. On the other hand, left like that, unattended, it would probably create panic and be (as they threatened constantly) 'destroyed'. She thought destruction was the more likely outcome; but she accepted she would probably never know. That was what Gurdjieff and Katherine, in a dream repeated over several nights, had instructed her to do: she was to contrive the end she wanted; but she was to leave the final outcome to chance.

What she liked to imagine was Max seeing it on television, her gift to him in the moments before it was covered by a protective hood and blown to bits—the yellow-striped bag reminding him of their picnic that summer in the fields and woods of Fontainebleau-Avon.

ALSO BY C.K. STEAD

POETRY

Whether the Will is Free
Crossing the Bar
Quesada
Walking Westward
Geographies
Poems of a Decade
Paris
Between
Voices
Straw into Gold
The Right Thing
Dog
The Red Tram
The Black River
Collected Poems 1951–2006
The Yellow Buoy

FICTION

CRITICISM

The New Poetic
In the Glass Case
Pound, Yeats, Eliot and the Modernist Movement
Answering to the Language
The Writer at Work
Kin of Place: Essays on 20 New Zealand Writers
Book Self: The Reader as Writer and the Writer as Critic
Shelf Life: Reviews, replies and reminiscences

AUTOBIOGRAPHY

South-West of Eden

EDITED

Oxford New Zealand Short Stories
Measure for Measure
Letters & Journals of Katherine Mansfield
Collected Stories of Maurice Duggan
Faber Book of Contemporary South Pacific Stories
Werner Forman's New Zealand